Celebrities Between The Sheets

SAVANNAH JAHVALL

CELEBRITIES BETWEEN THE SHEETS

2007

Celebrities Between The Sheets

CONTENTS

This Book Is Dedicated To You!

FOREWORD

Have you ever had a wild, erotic sex dream about your favorite celebrity? While you were dreaming, did it seem to be so real? You could feel the heat of his body against yours. Your arms and legs were wrapped around him, and then your body started to quiver. As you passionately kissed him, you tasted his tongue and felt it move gently all around your mouth. Your hips actually start to rock slowly back and forth in your bed; the sex is so real that you can almost feel him inside you. It is so good that you can feel yourself about to climax. It gets better and better, and then...your eyes start to open. You realize it was just a dream, leaving you hot and mad as hell. Damn, it was just a dream, and worse, you try to fall back asleep and finish where you left off, but it is too late, you are wide awake and can't get this dream out of your mind.

Do fantasies get any hotter than this? They do when the person you are dreaming about is your favorite celebrity. We all have dreamt about or thought what it would feel like to sleep with the ultimate sexy celebrity. Since I have been intimate with many of the hottest, sexiest men in the entertainment industry, I can tell you.

I will share all the juicy details of what it is really like to be intimate with a famous celebrity. I will reveal how big their member is, how long they lasted, how they kissed, smelled and tasted. I'll tell you the ones who had special, unusual interests or if they were just damn freaky. Now you too, can know who were the good ones, the minute men, Mandingos, and the romantics.

I won't give away the names, but don't worry! The description I provide will be so vivid, that by the end of each chapter, you will know who I am talking about. So, let's see how quickly you can guess who. If you have ever dreamed about sleeping with you favorite celebrity, here is a peek. I invite you into my world, where fantasies are reality.

CHAPTER 1
Sugar Daddy

One night, I was inside Dublin's one of the hottest sports bars on Sunset Boulevard. I went there with one of my celebrity friends named Ray J that I had known for about a year. We drove up to the club in a Cadillac Escalade Limousine. As soon as we arrived, we received VIP treatment. We went directly to the front of the line and we were immediately seated inside the VIP area. We ordered a bottle of Cristal and we checked out the crowd. It was halfway packed, so it was kind of easy to see who was there.

I suddenly noticed that over by the entrance there were a lot of people crowding around a 7 ft tall, about 300 lb, dark, familiar man. I recognized him, he is one of the most dominant players in the NBA, and he played for the Los Angeles Lakers as a center. People were shaking his hand, and the females were crowding around him breaking their necks to get close enough to talk to him. It was like watching the entrance of a king. He started pushing himself through the crowd and began walking toward the VIP section in which we were sitting. He looked over at our table and noticed my friend, who then motioned for him to come and sit with us. The crowded celebrity made his way over to our table and sat down. He shook hands with my friend and said, "What's up, hommie?"

I looked at him, smiled, and said hi. He turned to my friend and he asked, "Is she with you?"

He said, "No, this is my friend, Savannah." We shook hands, and right away he asked, "Do you have a man?" I said, "Not at the moment."

He said, "Good, do you have a two-way?"

"Yes, why?"

"Let me see it."

I pulled the two-way from my purse and handed it to him. He put my contact information in his two-way and then handed it back to me. He said, "I will call you soon, just make sure you answer the phone when I call." He then gave me a hug, and walked off with his boys.

"What is he like?" I asked Ray after he was gone. He told me he was real cool, and he loves to take care of his females very nicely. I had heard that about him before, which was fine with me, but I wasn't sure if he would really call because I knew he got a lot of attention and phone numbers from many different women.

Three days later, I was hanging out with my girls when my cell phone rang. I picked up the phone and heard a really deep voice say, "Hello, may I speak to Savannah?"

"This is she, who is this?"

"You should know who this is, it's Daddy."

I smiled. I knew exactly who it was. I was so excited that he called. "How are you, Daddy?" I said.

"Good, but I would be better if you don't have any plans for tonight."

"No, I have nothing planned, why? Do you want to see me?"

"Of course, why don't you come over to my house, if you are not busy?"

"I'll come over, where do you live?" I took down the directions, and I asked him what time he would like me to be there.

He said, "I want you to be here at 8:00 p.m., and when you get to the gate, tell the guard that you are here to see the King."

"The King?" I asked.

"Yeah, they'll know who you are talking about. Just tell them."

"Okay, I will see you soon."

I hung up the phone and suddenly became very nervous. My stomach started turning, and I just stood there for a second. Then it hit me. I was really going over to this man's house. I was not really sure why I was that nervous; I had been with celebrities before, so why was I tripping? Maybe it was the way people treated him like a king that made me feel like I was on my way to a palace.

I immediately got in the shower and began to get ready. I put on a short tight skirt and a low cut top that showed my cleavage to make him say, "Damn, you look good." I put my hair in a sexy up-do style, and made sure my makeup was flawless. I stood in front of the mirror and checked myself from head to toe. I made sure everything was just right before I went out the door. I felt perfect. I was ready for my evening with Daddy.

As I was driving closer to his house, I was getting nervous again. I had to tell myself not to be nervous. I could not help it, I didn't know what to say or do when I got there. Should I sleep with him on the first night? Okay, I should stop tripping and just go with the flow.

I approached the gate at the entrance where he lived. There was a small, square, peach-colored security booth with the guard inside. The guard looked at me and asked, "What is your name, and who are you here to see?" I told him that I was here to see Daddy, and he then picked up a phone. I could hear the guard telling someone that Savannah was here and asking permission to let me through the gate. He then handed me a map and gave me directions on how to get to the house.

I slowly drove through the entrance, and said to myself out loud, "Please don't get lost and look like an idiot driving around this nice neighborhood." It was almost 8 o'clock at night, and the streetlights gleamed down on the beautiful homes with perfectly manicured lawns. They all had nice cars in the driveways, and I couldn't help but notice how quiet it was.

I found his house with no problem, and I parked my car in front of it. This was a big house! It was nicely landscaped. His logo of an "S" was embedded into the ground, and into the front door. I walked up to the huge, tall door and rang the bell. He answered the door immediately; I felt overwhelmed. Damn, he is huge! He smiled and in a big, deep, sexy voice, he said, "Hey, sexy!" With his huge hands he picked me up, gave me a hug and kissed me on my lips. As I walked down the hallway, he started showing me around the house. It was really nice. It had three levels. We took the elevator to the first floor, which had a game room with pool tables, video machines, and a bar. There were bedrooms further down the hall, for the maid and chef.

We got back into the elevator and took it to the second floor, where the house was open and spread out. It made you feel very comfortable. His dining room table was so big and long it could easily seat twenty people. The kitchen had marble counter tops and a great view of the mountains. It really was like a palace.

The third level of the house had a long open hallway with lots of bedrooms. I walked into his black and white decorated bedroom, which had a huge round bed in the center.

The curtains opened and closed by a remote control. He had a gigantic flat screen television and a walk-in closet that was every girl's dream.

After he gave me the tour of the house, we walked downstairs to the kitchen. His personal chef was waiting there to make us dinner. When I was introduced to him, he immediately asked, "What can I make you?"

"What are my choices?" Before I began an answer we were interrupted.

"Make her shrimp scampi, fresh garden salad, and baked chicken," Daddy ordered. While the chef was preparing dinner, we talked and joked around a lot. He again asked if I was seeing anyone, and I told him I wasn't. His expression became serious. "Okay, good, understand that I do not like my business in the streets, so let's keep this between me and you."

I never asked him if he was seeing anyone, because that would have been a dumb question. I knew, of course he was. I really didn't care how many people he was seeing, as long as we were having safe sex, and he was treating me good. Dinner was finally ready, and I must say everything looked so good. Thomas was an excellent chef!

After dinner we headed upstairs to the master suite. As I walked in the door, he turned on some romantic music, and we relaxed on the bed. I was lying on my back and he was on his side. He took his hand, and put it on my back and pulled me against his body. His hand moved from the bottom of my back to my neck. He gently moved my head toward his lips. I placed my right hand on the back of his head, and began to kiss him. I have to say, he was a good kisser. His lips and tongue were very soft, and he knew how to move his tongue very well. He put his tongue against mine and moved it slowly in a circular motion. He then gently bit my bottom lip and placed his tongue in my mouth again. We were still kissing, when he lifted my shirt. He put his hand on my left nipple and lightly rubbed it. It felt so good that the hair on my arms stood up. He stopped kissing me, and he moved down the bed and took my left breast in his mouth and gently licked and sucked it. I wrapped my legs around his waist and took his shirt off him. I pulled it over his head and dropped it on the bed. He moved down and started to kiss me on my stomach, lower and lower, until he reached the top of my clitoris. He touched it with the tip of his tongue, and then he would stop and touch it again, teasing me, driving me crazy. Now, he was licking it up and down fast. My shaking legs were wrapped around his head, while my nails were digging in his shoulders. I was moaning and moving my hips around, I could not keep still. He would not stop. My heart was pounding so fast and I could feel myself about to climax. "You're going to make me cum," I told him. He said, "I know, go ahead."

I could not hold it in anymore. I dug my nails hard into his shoulders and groaned "I'm cuming now!" My whole body was shaking, and I told him to stop, but he kept on licking it. I took my legs, pushed down on his shoulders, and moved him off me. I moved all the way back on the bed and he grabbed my legs and pulled me toward him. I was very curious to know what he was working with. Since he was so tall and big, I expected it to be huge. So I grabbed his boxer shorts, and I pulled them down. To my surprise, it was just average. I would guess it was six to seven inches long, two inches in width, dark, and it had a nice rim. He reached for a condom from the nightstand, ripped it open and began to put it on. He laid me on my back and put his body on top of mine lightly, so he wouldn't crush me. Passionately, we started French kissing again. I placed my hands on his lower back and moved them all the way up his hard firm body, over his shoulders, then moved them back down his stomach, until I reached his manhood. It was as hard as a rock. I began to put it inside me, and he pushed it all the way in until he reached my G-spot. He moved it in and out very slowly, and then in a circular motion. My mouth was right at his chest so I was gently biting, and licking around his nipple. He was moaning, and the sweat from his body was all over mine. He put his left hand under my ass, and with that one hand he began to move my hips up and down on his dick very fast, while his body was stiff and straight. All I have to say is it was incredible! It was like he was Superman. I just relaxed my body and effortlessly enjoyed it.

As he was moving me up and down on himself, he asked me, "Who's your Daddy?"

I answered, "Daddy you are." He was moving me so fast, that my breasts were bouncing all around my chest, and the bed was shaking so hard I thought it was going to break. He was sweating so profusely that my whole body was covered with it.

He was pumping harder and suddenly he moaned, "I'm cumming." I wrapped my legs around him so he could not move. All of a sudden, he started shaking and he bit his bottom lip. My sexy Daddy lifted his head back in the air and let out a deep, loud moan. Then he laid his hot, sweaty body on top of me for a few minutes. I rubbed his back until he finally got off me. We stayed in bed and talked for a while, until we fell asleep.

When I opened my eyes it was morning already. I rolled over and kissed him on his lips. He smiled at me and said, "I'm ready for round two."

After the second round of sex, we got into the shower together and played around. We ended up having a soap fight;

soap bubbles were everywhere. We were covered in them, and ended up using the whole bottle. We washed each other from head to toe, and then finished the soapy shower and got dressed. We went downstairs to have some breakfast, and when we got to the kitchen his friends were already eating. He introduced me to his friends. They seemed friendly and polite. We sat down, and told the chef what we wanted for breakfast. We ordered waffles, eggs, and turkey bacon. Everything was made fresh, and it was fantastic. I noticed there was a yellow cake with chocolate frosting on the counter, I asked him if I could have a slice. He said "Sure, but be careful. Once you taste it, you will be hooked."

I took a bite of it. The cake was so good that it melted in my mouth. This was the best cake I had ever tasted. His chef really was remarkable.

During breakfast, he mentioned that he had to go to a charity event and needed to leave soon. I said no problem. Daddy asked me, "Do you need some money to get your hair done, since I messed it up?"

"Yes, you did do a good job messing it up!"

He smiled, "Do you need money for anything else?"

I looked at him and said, "Sure."

Daddy said, "How much do you need?"

"It does not matter," I said.

"That's not what I asked you, how much do you need?"

I did not know what to say, I did not want to say too high of an amount and look like a gold digger, so I said, "Well, I do have some bills to pay, is $5,000 too much?"

He said, "Okay, I will be right back."

He left the kitchen and came back with $5,000 in cash. "Here you go, I love to take care of my girls, and I want to make sure you're comfortable." I thanked him for the money and gave him a hug and a kiss.

Daddy said it was time for him to leave, so he walked me to my car, gave me a kiss and told me he would call. He and his friends then left on their motorcycles, and I drove home. He called me quite a bit after that unforgettable night, and we did hang out quite often.

Daddy was more than I expected. He is a lot of fun and he has a wonderful sense of humor. He loves to take care of his women and he is very generous. His body, I would say is an eight, only because it is not cut up. The sex was very good; he knows what he is doing and has great moves. I will give the sex a nine. The whole experience is a nine plus. He is definitely a keeper. He treated me the way a woman should be treated. I wish more men were like him!

CHAPTER 2
The Two Minute Man

Okay, it will take you about two minutes to read this chapter, and hopefully you won't be as disappointed as I was. For those of you who like quickies, you will truly enjoy this; for those of you who don't, you will understand my frustration. Let me explain.

I was at my friend's house in Culver City, sitting in front of the fireplace having a drink. It was a Saturday night and we had just eaten at The Stinking Rose. We decided to go back to his house and relax for the rest of the evening. He mentioned that his brother played for the NBA Clippers as a small forward. I had never met him before, and he wanted to introduce me to him. "Well, where is he?" I said. "He is in his room, I'll call him." He yelled out his brother's name, "Yo C" and a door in front of us opened. A huge shadow peeked out. Then a golden, absolutely gorgeous man, wearing nothing but a pair of tight, black boxers walked into the room. God damn, he looked good. His body was perfect. Every single muscle was firm, tight, and cut up almost like it was sculpted to perfection. The muscles in his lower abdomen were so defined, I gasped quietly at the sight. His skin was smooth and creamy, like hot caramel. He had nice, big sexy lips, the kind that makes you just want to kiss them all the time. His eyes were shaped slightly tight and sexy looking. He was remarkable!

He walked over to me, and he bent down to shake my hand, "How are you?" he asked.

I smiled and gave him a look that said I want you. He walked into the kitchen to get a drink of water. I watched him drink every last drop while thinking to myself I would love to drink him. He walked back into his bedroom, and my eyes went with him until he shut his bedroom door. Damn, I wanted that!

I turned to my friend and said, "You have got to hook me up with your brother? He is fine."

"All right, let me see what's up." He went into his brother's room to talk with him. About two minutes went by, and then he came back out. He said, "You can go in his room, it's cool."

By that time, I had gotten some liquor in me and I felt really nice. I was ready to get my freak on. I could hardly wait to lick every inch of him and kiss those sexy lips. I was ready to tear him up.

I got up and headed to his brother's room. I opened the door, and he was laying on his bed with the lights dim and the radio playing. He said, "Take off your clothes."

Oh shit, it's on and cracking! I thought to myself. As I was taking off my clothes, I saw him get a condom out of the drawer. As he started to put it on, I noticed that his penis was kind of small, about five inches long. Hmm, I thought to myself, I hope he does not disappoint me! But as fine as he is, and if he knows how to work it, then it's all good.

My clothes were off and I straddled my legs around his thighs. We began to tongue kiss each other and I was starting to get really hot. My pussy was getting so wet. I decided I was ready to get on top of him. I wanted to ride him like crazy until I climaxed. I put it inside me and I moved up and down for about two minutes. All of a sudden, I hear him making an unexpected noise. "Uhhh!" No, this fine man didn't just cum. I was just getting started! No! No! No! Damn it, tell me he did not just bust one!

I hate to admit it, but friends, yes he did. I am not exaggerating this, it was done and over. That was it, that's all he had to offer. I really thought I was going to have a nice sexual flight, but damn, the flight fifty landed in two minutes flat!

A few girls that I know had also slept with him, and they said the same thing: he climaxes really fast! So, it wasn't just me. That is just how he is. What a shame. He is too damn fine to be coming that quick. Is it because he is so quick on the court that he is quick in bed, too? What a disappointment!

I hate to do this to him, but sadly he is going to get a three for this rating. I would give him a two, because he only gave me two minutes of him. Only because he is oh so fine, I will give him one free throw point higher. I'm sorry but two minutes is just not enough for me. Everything else is cool about him. He just needs to learn how to last longer. Then, he would be good to perfect!

CHAPTER 3
Unpredictable

One night, I had stopped by one of my friend's house to find out if anything was going on for the evening. My friend, whom I was visiting, was a lesbian so there were always women over at her house just hanging out, both straight and gay. It was a cool spot to kick it and just chill out. I never had to call her and ask if I could stop by, I would just show up and it was cool.

When I walked in the door, she had three of her friends there. The music was loud, and they were dancing in the living room having a good time. Drinks were being made, they were taking ecstasy, and the blunt was being passed around. She introduced me to her friends, and made me a drink.

We were all lounging on her bed, just talking and smoking. My friend and her girl were lying next to each other, kissing. One of the girls said, "Is there somewhere we can go and hang out, because I don't feel like watching them get their freak on all night?"

"Not that I can think of, there are no clubs going on, and I have not heard of any parties either. Maybe we should call some guys to come over and chill with us."

"There is really no one that I want to see."

"There has to be something that we can do. Oh yeah, I know who I can call, my boy Jay. Hopefully, he is home, and we can go over there and hang out," I said.

"Who are you talking about?"

"Hold on, let me call him before I tell you." I picked up the phone, dialed the number, and it was ringing.

"Hello."

"Hey, it's Savannah, do you feel like having five fine looking females over your house tonight?"

"Five of you, and there fine, and are they down?"

"Yeah, they are straight, you'll like them, and they are definitely with it."

"That's real cool, because a few of my boys are over here right now, and we have no plans. So we can have a little get together. Come through in about an hour."

"All right, we will be there in about an hour." I hung up the phone, and I told the girls that we could go over there and hang out.

"Who are you talking about, you never told us?"

"He is a famous comedian named _ _ _ _ _, you know the one who has the comedy television show on the WB Network, and he also sings and plays the piano very well. You can see him playing football on any given Sunday. He is tall, dark and a fox." After I told them who it was, they got all excited and said, "Oh hell yeah, I want to go. I would love to fuck the shit out of him."

The other girl said, "I know, I have always had a thing for him. Let's go, I'm ready."

I looked at them. "You guys are definitely his type, so I know it will go down tonight." I told all the girls, "We need to get one thing straight before we leave. He loves to have sex, and it probably will go down, so if any of you are not comfortable with this type of situation, then you should not go. I do not want to get over there and have to hear I want to go home. I'm driving, so you guys have to stay until I am ready to go."

They all said they wanted to go and hang out with him. My friend said, "I want to go, but you know that I only do girls, so I won't be doing anything, is it still cool to go?"

"That's fine, I just don't want him to hear anyone complaining. He and I are real cool with each other, and he will pull me aside and ask why I brought you girls over here, if you aren't comfortable with the situation. Don't get me wrong, anyone can always go over there and just hang out. You don't have to do anything with him; he's not like that. It's that he just does not want to hear any whining or complaining."

She said, "That's cool. I understand, let's go."

We left her spot, and headed for his house. When we walked up to the gate, the door was locked. I rang the bell. He could see who we were, because there is a security camera looking right at us. One of his friends came out and opened the door for us. "Hey ladies, come on in." He gave me a kiss on my cheek and walked us thru the kitchen door. His friend said,

"Have a seat and I will go get Jay."

We sat down at the round glass table, and one of the girls said, "I can't wait to see him, I'm so nervous."

I replied, "Just chill, he's real cool and he will make you feel so comfortable that you will forget who he is."

He and four of his boys walked into the kitchen, and I got up and gave him a big hug. He opened his arms wide and said, "Come give me a hug, ladies. Don't be scared, I'm not gonna bite you, unless you want me to. I'm just kidding. What are your names?" They all got up one by one, and gave him a hug and introduced themselves to him and the other guys. He said, "Who wants drinks, because I make a mad secret mixed drink that will get you faded?"

We all said, "Yes, please make us some drinks."

Except for one of my girls who said, "None for me, I'm the

designated driver for tonight, so can you make me something else?"

Jay said, "I can do that, but you have to just taste it, because these are really good."

"Okay, I'll taste it since you are going out of your way to make us your secret drink."

While Jay was making the drinks, he said, "I have an idea. Are you guys down to play a game?"

I said, "What do you have in mind?"

"Let's play a drinking game; we can play the guys against the girls. Here are the rules. You have to take this quarter and bounce it off the table, and try to get it in this shot glass. If you make it you get to pick someone from the opposite team, and they have a choice to either drink the shot or take something off. Are you down or scared?"

One of the guys responded, "I'm a grown ass man, dawg, you know I can handle it. I think the ladies are afraid that they will lose and end up butt naked."

"Please, the only one that is going to lose their clothes are ya'll. You have no idea how much we can drink," I said.

"She's right, I have seen her drink, and she can hold hers, but what about the rest of you ladies?" Jay asked.

"We will find out soon enough. Bring it on," one of the girls said. He brought the drinks to the table, and he had one of his boys get some more chairs. When the chairs were brought in, he told us to sit in boy—girl order.

My girl asked, "Can I go first?"

Jay replied, "Go on with your fine self, take the shot!"

She put the quarter in her hand, aimed it at the shot glass, and bounced it on the table. "Cling," she made it right in the shot glass. All of us girls put our hands in the air and started yelling, "Oh, it's on now, who's gonna take the first drink of the night?"

My girl said, "I think the man of the house should take the first drink. Are you scared, or do you need me to help you?"

"Whaaat scared? Girl, you don't know who you are messing with! I am the king of this game, but since you offered to help me, why don't you come over here, and give me some assistance." My girl got up from her seat, and walked around the table, picked up the shot glass, and held it up to his lips. He tilted his head back, and she poured it in.

One of his friends said, "Ahh, I think I need a little help too, can someone pick me next, I think I need some assistance."

She sat back down in her seat, and she passed the quarter and shot glass to the guy sitting next to her.

"All right, one of you ladies is going to be drinking right about now." He took the shot, and he made it. He jumped up and started doing the "Cabbage Patch Dance." He pointed to one of the girls, and said, "Drink, I want you to drink, and drink every last drop of it."

She agreed. "No problem, this is a piece of cake." She took the glass and drank the whole thing in one shot. The guy looked at her and said, "Damn, you girls really ain't no joke, I thought you would be sipping on it, and making faces, but I see that you are a G. We are really going to have some competition up in here. But there is no way that we are going to let some females beat us in a drinking game!"

"Okay, keep talking shit, you are going to be the first one throwing up!" she said.

He gave me the quarter, and I took my turn. I missed. "Damn it. Give me the drink so I can get this over with."

Jay said, "You don't have to drink, you can take something off if you like. As a matter of fact, why don't you take off your shirt?"

I laughed, "I bet you would love for me to do that, but not yet. You know that I can hang, we have been through this before."

He smiled at me and said, "Yup, and we are about to go through it again. You will be naked by the end of the night!"

"And so will you," I said. I took the drink with no problem, and I slid the quarter over to Jay.

"Are you ladies ready to drink?" He took the shot and made it.

"Shit," I said, "Who are you going to pick?"

He slid the glass over to me and laughed. I knew he was going to pick me. "I just got done taking a shot, pick one of them."

"Nope, drink up or take it off," he said.

"Okay, okay, give me the drink." So I took another drink.

"Are you ready to quit yet?"

"Hell no, you will quit before I do," I said.

He slid the quarter to the girl sitting next to him. "It's your turn, sexy."

She bounced the quarter on the table, and she missed it. The guys were yelling, "Take something off!"

She said, "As a matter of fact, I will." She took off her shirt, and she was not wearing a bra, her nipples were pink and erect.

One of the guys said, "Yeah, that's what I'm talking about, I want to see all you ladies take it off."

The guy next to her took his turn. He missed it, and he decided that he was going to drink. It was now one of the ladies' turn. She bounced it on the table, and she made it. "Yes," she pointed to Jay and said, "Drink up honey, drink up."

"With pleasure." He took the shot glass, drank it, and slammed the glass on the table! "I can keep doing this all night!" he exclaimed. "Who is next?"

"Me, Dawg, and I am not gonna miss, so the girl in the red top, get ready to drink." He took the shot, and he missed.

"All that shit you were talking, and you miss! Drink up," the girl in the red top said.

"No, I think I will take something off," he told her. Then, he took off his shirt.

One of the girls said, "I thought you were going to show us more than that, why don't you take off your pants?"

"Nope, that's all you're gonna get for now, next person go."

One of the girls took her turn, and she missed. "What you gonna do, are you going to drink or take it off? It's peer pressure, drink or take it off, drink or take it off?"

"Oh all right, I'll take it off." So she stands up, and she starts to give them a strip show while she is taking off her shirt. The guys were whistling and cheering. She took off her shirt, and she had on a red lacy bra.

Jay said, "I like that, but I can't wait to see what is under it." She sat back down, and the guy next to her took his turn. He aimed for the shot glass, and he made it. He looked at me, and he said, "Drink or take it off."

I said, "Give me the drink." I took the drink to the head in one sip.

Jay whispered in my ear, "I know you're getting faded, so you might as well take it off, so we can go to the room."

I said, "No, when you take it off, then I will take it off, but until then, I'm gonna keep drinking."

"Okay, don't get sick," he said.

"Never that."

It was my friend's turn again, and she made it in. I looked at her and I said, "Please, make Jay drink. All this shit he's talking, he needs to be taught a lesson."

"I agree, drink up, or shut up," she said.

"Shut up," he says smiling. "I have something that will make you shut up." He stood up and took off his shirt.

The girls yelled, "Finally, take it off!" He pulled his shirt over his head, and his six-pack, was spectacular. We were thinking that he was about to sit back down, when he began taking off his pants too. He slid his pants and his draws off, and he was standing there butt-ass naked. His dick was swinging back and forth, and he started jumping up and down.

"Damn, you have a big, pretty looking dick," one of the girls shouted out.

Another girl said, "Let's go in the other room, enough of this game."

"Shit, you don't have to ask me twice, follow me down the hall to my studio" Jay said.

We all got up from the table and followed him thru the living room, down the hallway, and into the studio. He opened the door and dimmed the lights. Some of us sat down on the couch, some were leaning on the wall, and a few sat down on the floor. We all knew it was about to go down. I was waiting to see how the girls were going to react. I could see the girls looking at him like, "Damn, I'm first."

Jay went toward one of the girls who was sitting on the floor, and he started rubbing on her ass. She took off her pants, turned around in a doggie style position, and stuck her ass out. He put a condom on and stuck his nine-inch dick in her and began fucking her from behind. We were all watching them, and everyone started getting turned on. The guys began taking down their pants and stroking their dicks. The girls took off all their clothes, and they were playing with themselves. One of the girls wanted a piece of Jay, so she got up from the couch, and laid on the ground next to the girl he was fucking. She was on her back, and her legs were open and she was rubbing on her nipples. He was looking at her, while he was still fucking the girl from behind. He then took his dick out of her, and he put it in the other girl. One of his friends started fucking the girl from whom he just pulled out. Both of them were fucking these girls for a while, when Jay pulled his dick out of the girl.

He got up and sat next to me on the couch. He took the condom off, and he started stroking himself up and down, with a sexy look on his face. Only the one couple was still fucking on the floor, while the rest of us were satisfying ourselves. Two of his boys were leaning against the wall stroking themselves, and Jay and his friend were sitting on the couch next to me stroking it up and down. Everyone was watching them have sex on the floor and watching each other pleasuring themselves. All of a sudden, at the same time, everyone in the room had an orgasm. I could hear ahs, and oh shit, and oh yeah, baby.

Jay said, "Now that's what's up. That was good. Does anyone need anything?"

"Can we take a shower?" one of the girls asked.

"Yeah, who ever wants to take a shower, follow me," Jay said. All five of us girls followed him to the shower. My girl and her girlfriend went in one bathroom, and the two remaining ones and I went into his master bathroom in his room. He had a nice size beautiful shower, so we all decided to get in there together and wash up. As the three of us girls were getting clean, Jay opened the door and got in with us. He took his hands, and he rubbed the soap on our chests, one by one. The girls loved it, and he knew it. One girl was stroking his dick, and the other one was behind him, rubbing on his ass. They could have done just about whatever they wanted to him, and he would not have cared. He gently pushed the girl who was stroking his dick down to her knees, and she began to give him head. The water was running all over them. The girl behind him, had both of her hands on his nipples rubbing them, and she was licking on his neck. I opened the shower door to let him be alone with the girls because I had been with him plenty of times before. So I was not tripping.

He said, "Where are you going?"

I told him, "I was going to let you be alone with the girls."

"No, I want you to stay. You know your shit is tight, and I want it. Go get a condom out of the nightstand."

I walked over to the nightstand, got the condom, opened the shower door, and I gave it to him. He opened it up and put it on. He turned me around, and took my hands and put them high up on the glass shower door. He spread my legs apart with his feet, and he put his nine-inch dick inside me. He was standing up fucking me from behind. The water was running all down my back, and he was bending his knees, while holding on to my waist, and moving his dick in and out of me as fast as he could. One girl was behind him, rubbing his balls, and the other girl was rubbing his chest. He just kept on pumping and pumping as hard as he could. The girl behind him pulled him off me, turned him around, grabbed his dick and started to put it in her. He loved it. He said to her, "Damn, you must really want some of this, so you better be able to take it."

She said, "Give it to me now."

He picked her up, and leaned her against the shower and started fucking the shit out of her. She was yelling and telling him, "Oh yeah, oh yeah, harder, harder." So he gave it to her hard and fast. I could tell that he needed more room, so I stepped out of the shower and left the three of them in there alone.

When I went into the kitchen, the other girls were in there sitting down at the table talking to the guys. They asked me, "Where are the three of them at?"

I told them that they were in the shower, and they might be a while. An hour went by, and they all walked into the room with big smiles on their faces. I said to the girls, "Are you guys ready to go?"

They said, "Yeah, we're ready if you are."

I walked over to my boy and I told him, "We're getting ready to head home, but thanks for showing us a good time, I really appreciate it. I'll give you a call soon."

He gave me a hug, kissed me on my cheek, and said, "Anytime." He gave the rest of the girls a hug, and we left.

There was another time some friends and I were at a pool party, which was boring as hell. Nobody was there, and we were ready to go. It was still early in the day and we did not want to go home. So I decided that I was going to call him up and see if we could come over. He said it was cool, and he was not doing anything. So we left the pool party and hit the freeway.

When we got to his house, he asked us if we wanted to go swimming. My girl and I said yes, but the other three girls said no. They were straight. He told us that he had some swimsuits in his bottom draw in his room. She and I went in his room and changed into the swimsuits. The other girls sat by the pool and had a drink. When we got outside, he was already naked in the pool. We jumped in the water, and we started swimming and playing around. We were trying to dunk each other under the water. I got out of the pool to take a sip of my drink. When I got back in, he was behind my girl with his arms around her, and she was holding onto a pool chair. He was standing behind her for a cool minute. I looked over at them more closely, and I could see him moving his hips back and forth in the pool slowly. He was trying to fuck her from behind. Go on with your bad self, I thought. He knew I didn't care. I didn't know if it bothered the other girls that were sitting by the pool, but I doubted if he really was concerned about what they thought. He was doing what he wanted to do in his own house, and that is how it should be. If anyone did not want to see it, they could have gotten up and gone in the house.

This man was a lot of fun to be with. I would absolutely love going to his house and just hanging out with him. We would shoot some hoops, chill in the Jacuzzi, and have some really good sex. Whenever I would bring my girls over there, he would always show them a good time. He would order us food; he made sure we had drinks, and he loved to entertain us.

He had a very nice body, and he always kept it in shape. Most of us girls would call him a fox, because of how he looked. From his head to his toes, he was nice and firm. He was about 5 ft 10 in. His skin was smooth and he had a nice medium-colored complexion. He definitely looked good. The ladies would be all over him, when we went out.

He was so unpredictable. He would have sex at any time. He did not care who was watching him. That was just how he was. It did not matter what race a female was, as long as she looked good, then, he would be with her. He was cool with everyone. He just loved to be around beautiful women, and he loved to have sex with them. The sex was good, and he knew how to work it. The size of his manhood was perfect. It was not too big, but not too small. I enjoyed it, and so did my friends.

All in all, I am going to give him an eight. Thanks for the memories and good times Jay. You're the best.

CHAPTER 4
Simply The Best

I knocked on the hotel door of the St. Regis Hotel, waiting anxiously for my New York Rapper to open the door. I could hear the music of his song playing loudly in the hallway, (hug me, love me, judge me, the only man that help is above me, holla). It was a song with him and a sexy Latina singer doing a duet together. "Who is it?" he says in a raspy voice.

"It's Savannah."

He opened the door and stood there wearing an open, white terry cloth robe and a pair of black Calvin Klein boxers. I could only see the P and L of his tattoo on his upper left chest. He said to me, "You're always on time."

He grabbed my hand, pulled me in the room, and closed the door. He took my purse from me, dropped it on the floor, and gently pushed me back on the bed. I was sitting on the bed, leaning back on my elbows, and looking intensely into his eyes. He immediately put his knees on the outside of my legs and put his hands on the side of my neck. He kissed me forcefully with his tongue. He moved his tongue against mine fast, but then he slowed it down. He took his mouth off my lips, and he began to kiss my cheek and forehead. His hands moved from my neck up into my hair, and he pulled it, making my head go back. He put his tongue on my neck, and he started sucking it hard while moving his tongue around slowly in a circle. Chills began to run down my back. He moved my head with his hand to the other side, and he licked it nice and slow. He let go of my hair and he stopped licking my neck.

He took his hands, placed them on my blouse, and pulled it open causing the buttons to pop off. He gently held my right breast in his hand and placed it in his mouth and licked my nipple up and down at a medium pace with the tip of his tongue. He moved his mouth over my breast as far as he could, and he began sucking it at the back of his throat, fast and then slow. He took my breast out of his mouth, and moved his tongue across my chest, and began to kiss my other nipple. He gently placed my nipple in between his teeth, and moved his tongue back and forth across it, while his hand traveled from my breast down the sides of my stomach, all the way until he reached my right inner thigh. As he moved his hand inside my thighs, he placed it on the outside of my black silk panties. His hand moved up and down while he gently squeezed my pussy. His finger moved my panties to the side, and he inserted it up inside my sugar walls. He finger-banged me slowly, moving his finger in and out while touching my clit with his thumb. He was moving his finger at the back of my G-Spot very fast. The pleasure of this was driving me crazy. I moved my hips back and forth, clenching the sheets. He took his finger out, he grabbed a hold of my panties, and he ripped them off me.

He moved my legs apart with his hands, and he began to eat me like crazy. He licked me all the way from my ass to the tip of my clit, in a circular motion. He then moved his tongue to my opening, and stuck it in as far as it would go and then took it out and moved it back to my clit. He again took his finger, and put it up inside me. I was getting the best of both worlds. He kept on licking me and finger-banging me, until I could not take it anymore. I couldn't hold back any longer, I grabbed his head and held onto his braids, while my body began to shake uncontrollably. I was having one of the best orgasms in my life. He was still licking me; he just wouldn't stop. He kept on going, and I was about to have another orgasm. I yelled, "Damn, it feels so good!"

He stopped and lifted his head. He stood up, pulled me off the bed, and turned me around. Then, he bent me forward on the bed, grabbed a condom, and put it on. He began to fuck me from behind. His hands were on my hips, while he quickly moved his eight-inch dick in and out of me. He was moving it in and out really fast. He grabbed my hair and gently pulled it back and slapped my ass. We fucked in this position for about twenty minutes. He took his dick out, and he rubbed it back and forth on the outside of my pussy. His dick moved across my clit a few times, and then he put it back inside me. He only had the tip in, and he moved it in a circular motion, while making a deep growling noise.

He then turned me around, and laid me on my back. He pushed my legs all they way back behind my head. His necklace was hitting me in the face, so I took it off his neck and dropped it on the bed. He grabbed my hands and pinned them down, so I could not move them. He was fucking me so hard and fast, that the mattress was sliding off the bed. He was kissing me so passionately with his tongue, and fucking me all wild that I could feel myself about to cum again. I did not want to cum again just yet, so I pushed him off me, and I laid him on his back.

I got on top of him, and I began to ride him real slow so that he would feel every muscle inside me. As I was riding him, he took his hands and pulled me forward until my breasts were pressed against his chest. He moved his hand down my back, and he grabbed my ass and moved it up and down on his dick. He kept on moving me up and down squeezing my ass tightly.

He leaned forward and picked me up and laid me on the floor. He was fucking me so good that I was digging my nails into his back. I suddenly felt him bite my arm. I was feeling pain, but I was also feeling pleasure from it. We were both moving our hips up and down fast, when he suddenly took his dick out, pulled off the condom, and jacked it off. He squirted his hot cum all over my stomach, and he hollered. Now, that's what I'm talking about.

This rapper here is off the chain. He knew how to put it on me. The way he kissed me, was passionate yet aggressive. He knew when to kiss me slowly, but then he knew when it was the perfect time to speed it up. The way he would take his hands and touch my body was incredible. He would lightly touch me and give me chills, but then he would bite me or grab me a little rough to spice it up. He would be making love to me so well, when all of a sudden he would turn it into a playful experience. Not painful, but rough as in, "Oh, yeah, baby, spank me from the back and pull my hair." He would do it just right. The sex would last just long enough, not too quick, but not too long.

He always smelled so good. I don't know what cologne he used, but, whatever it was, it made me want to just smell him, then rip off his clothes and fuck the shit out of him.

His looks and personality were so cute; they were rugged, yet sexy. His skin was a caramel color; he wore a light moustache, and was not that tall. He also just started his career in acting.

The way he would always lay his head in my lap, take his arms and hold my legs, was so damn cute to me. I have to give him a ten. Now he is a must! If you run in to him, you have got to try it. He will put it on you!

CHAPTER 5
Gimme Some More

It was the morning of the first Sunday of the month. I called my friend Lori to see if she wanted to go with me to get a new outfit for the "Industry First Sunday" monthly event. She said, "You know I will, I have to look good for tonight, because it's going to be on, and with all those celebrities that are going to be there, I have to make sure I am looking good. Do not forget to call Dave to get our names on the list, so we won't have to wait in that long line."

I had called Dave Brown, who was one of the two people who gave the event. I asked him if he could put my name, plus one, on the list. He honored my request, but warned me it would be a madhouse. He told me to arrive early because he was hosting the official after-party of the NBA All-Star Game. We were all set as far as the list goes, now all we had to do was make sure we were looking damn good.

The Industry First Sunday monthly events were legendary! I don't know how to explain it, but the parties that they use to throw were so live and off the chain, it was ridiculous. When the first Sunday of the month arrived, everyone could not wait to get to the club. The events were so exclusive, that every month it would be held at a different location. If it was the first Sunday of the month, we all knew not to miss it, because if we did we would hear about it the next morning, and we would be mad as hell once we heard who was there and how good it was. Dave always invited so many celebrities to their events. Even the celebrities that did not live in L.A., that were in town on business, knew about First Sundays and they showed up there, too.

The guest had to arrive very early in order to get in. If it started at 10:00 p.m., they should have really arrived by 9:00 p.m. If they even thought about getting there at 10:00 p.m., they would be at the back of a very long line, and they would be there for a while before they would get in. I have seen it where the club would be at capacity by 11:00 p.m., and they were not letting anyone else in. That's how popular these events were.

I had forgotten that it was an NBA event going on, so I really needed to make sure that I was looking extra good. I called my hairdresser to see if she could fit me in. She told me that if I could get there within the next hour she could do it. Thank God she had an opening, because I was not trying to do my own hair. I left right away and headed for Chuck Taylor Barber and Hair. When I got there, "Daddy," who you read about in chapter one, was already sitting in the chair getting his hair cut by Chuck. I looked at him and smiled, and he smiled back. I did not go up to him and give him a hug due to the fact that we were keeping our relationship on the down low. I would often see him there, as well as many other NBA players getting their hair cut by Chuck. While I was getting my hair done, I could hear people either saying they'd be at the event or asking who was going.

When "Daddy" was finished getting his hair cut, he walked up to my hairdresser and gave her some money. "Here, this is for her hair."

I smiled and said, "Thanks." He is such a sweetie!

I had my hairdresser put my hair in an up-do style, with a little bit of hair hanging out around the edges. I chose to wear it that way, because it made me look really sexy, and that was the effect I wanted for the evening. My hair was done, and it was almost 3:00 p.m.

Since I was going to Beverly Hills to buy an outfit, I decided to call my friend who works at "Mac" to see if she could do my makeup. She had time, so that was one less thing that I had to worry about.

I called Lori and I told her I was on my way. When I arrived at her house, we headed straight for Beverly Hills. It was starting to get late, so we really needed to hurry and find something to wear. We found some sexy outfits that we liked, so we were set to go back to her place to get ready for the night.

We turned the radio on, and made us a drink, and started getting prepared. We looked damn good, I must say. It was time to go, so we got into the car and left for the club.

When we were in the car approaching the club, we noticed that there were quite a few limousines parked near it. It was already crowded, and the night was still early. The line to the valet parking was long. We waited for them to park the car for about ten minutes. It was about 9:30 p.m. by the time we started heading towards the club.

As we were walking, we could hear the music from the club playing loudly. The line to get in the club was so long it was ridiculous. It was down the street and around the corner. My girl said, "Can't we go to the front since we are on the list?"

"Yeah, we can, but look how crowded it is around the guy who has the list. Getting to him is going to be a bitch!"

People were pushing each other just so they could get to the security guard. Everyone was yelling, "I'm on the list, can you check for my name?"

The security guy was hollering, "I'm not letting anyone else in until you guys make a line!" It was out of control.

All of a sudden, a limo pulled up and security said, "Move back, I need everyone to move back now."

Nobody wanted to move because they did not want to lose their spot, so the security started moving us and making some space. That way the person inside the limo would have room to walk through the crowd. The limo door opened, and Mary J Blige got out. She walked right past everyone and immediately entered the club.

This was crazy! We needed to find a way to get inside, so I tried to call Dave on his cell phone to see if he could come out and get us, but he was not answering. I was like what the hell are we going to do. By now it was about 10:00 p.m., and no progress was being made. Finally, the security started looking around the crowd and picking people he wanted to come into the club. He looked over at us, and he asked, "What's your name?" I replied, "Savannah, plus one."

He looked at the list. "Okay, come on." He grabbed my hand and pulled us through the crowd. Finally, we were in!

We got a wristband, which gave us access to the VIP area. As soon as we turned the corner, Lori says "Shit, it is packed up in here!" There were people everywhere. You could barely walk through the crowd. The heat inside the club was intense. I was starting to sweat, and I had only been inside for a few minutes. We wanted to go the bar and get ourselves some drinks, but there were too many people crowded around it. We did not feel like waiting, so we decided to walk around and see who was there.

When we looked around we saw so many celebrities that it was ridiculous. There were NBA players, rappers, singers, and actors. I remember seeing Allen Iverson, Jamie Foxx, Juvenile, Shaq, Latrell Sprewell, and Ja Rule, just to name a few. They were all over the place, in the VIP area, at the bar, dancing, and partying.

The music was loud, the dance floor was packed, and everyone was having a good time. All of a sudden, the DJ started playing "Back That Azz Up," and the crowd went wild. The girls started backing that ass up and the guys were behind them dancing directly on their ass. People were holding their drinks in the air and dancing throughout the club. The celebrities were dancing with us and having a good time. Nobody cared who they were, everyone was there to party and get their drink on.

My girl and I were dancing together near the dance floor, when all of a sudden I felt someone come up behind me and he starts dancing right on my ass. I turned around to see who it was, and I was like, damn, he is fine. It was a sexy man who made most women go crazy. He was about six feet tall, with short black hair, and he had sexy, piercing, brown eyes. He was wearing a black silk shirt that was halfway unbuttoned and a pair of jeans that fit just right. I started dancing with him really close. Our hips were right against one another, and we were grinding each other so close, that I could feel his manhood. His shirt was open so I could see his sweaty, hard muscles. In my head I was thinking, *oh, how I want to feel them, but I wonder if he would trip if I touched them.* So, I said to myself, *what the hell just do it and see how he reacts.* I took both hands and I placed them on his chest, and I waited for his reaction, but he just kept on dancing while he was looking at my hands on his chest. So, I started to move my hands all around them and then down his stomach. His chest was hard as a rock, and his muscles on his six-pack were so tight and firm. They were rippling hot and sweaty. He then took his hands and placed them on my hips and started to move his sexy body all over me. Our bodies were so close, that when we looked at each other, our lips were almost touching. We stared into each other's eyes until the song was over.

When we stopped dancing, he asked me if my girl and I wanted to come to his table and have some champagne. I told him I would love to. So I grabbed my girl's hand, and we went to his table. We all sat down with his boys and a few other girls who were already there. He poured us each a glass of Cristal, we were just talking and having a good time. While we were talking, girls were coming up to the table to shake his hand and to introduce themselves to him. It didn't bother me at all. It comes with the territory when you are around a celebrity. I guess after watching him on a soap opera everyday, and now he was within a few feet from them, it might be the girls' only chance to say something to him. He was polite to them and shook their hands and said hello. At the same time, he was not disrespectful to me. After an hour went by, my girl wanted to go and dance some more, so I told him we were going to go to the dance floor. He said, "Give me your phone number, so I can call you if I don't see you later on tonight." I wrote it down for him, and he commented, "Okay, it was nice to meet you. Hopefully, I will see you before you leave, if not, I will call you." My girl and I went back to the dance floor.

While we were dancing, Dave motioned for us to come over to his table. When we got over to where he was sitting, he told us to sit down and have a drink. "I want you two to meet my friend Jay. Jay, this is Savannah and Lori this is Jay." (Jay is not his real name, but close to it).

Jay asked, "So how long have you known D?"

I replied, "About a year."

D turned and whispered in my ear, "You know who he is, right?"

I softly said, "Yeah, he has his own comedy television show."

"Well, we are having an after-party at his house. Why don't you two come over and hang out?"

"Okay, we might do that," I told him.

D said, "Well, you have my cell number; just call me and I will give you directions." "All right, we probably will come by."

Jay added, "You have to come over and check out my pad, I will personally make sure you girls have a good time."

I said, "Okay, we will be there. What time is it going to start?"

"We are going straight to the house when it is over, so anytime after the club is fine. Help yourself to some Champagne." While we were sitting with them, I saw one of my friends, who is really pretty, walk by our table, so I called her name and she looked over at us and waved.

Jay asked me, "Is that your friend?"

I said, "Yeah, do you want to meet her?"

"Tell her to come here."

So I got up from the table, and I walked up to her and I told her, "Jay wants to meet you. Come over and have a drink with us, and I'll introduce you to him." I brought her over to the table, and Jay immediately stood up and shook her hand. He took her to the other end of the table so they could talk in private. Next thing I knew, I saw them get up from the table and started dancing together.

D said, "You have to bring her with you tonight back to Jay's house. Make sure you make it happen for me."

"I will do my best; I'll find out what her plans are after the club."

Lori said to me, "Let's go walk around while they are dancing, and we will come back in a few minutes." We were walking around the club, when all of a sudden this tall, dark, fine NBA player touched Lori's arm. So, she stopped and talked to him for a few minutes. He asked her what she was doing after the club. She told him that we were going to Jay's house for an after-party.

"I might stop by. I know where he lives," the player commented.

"So you have been there before?"

"Yeah, you should go and check out his crib, you will have fun over there, and maybe we can get in the Jacuzzi together."

"Take down my number, and call me when you get there my name is Lori."

After he left, I said to her, "He is tall, dark, and chocolate, I know you want to go over there tonight, and kick it with him."

Lori responded, "Let's go and check it out, it sounds like it is going to be fun."

We went back to Dave's table, and I told him that we would be at Jay's house after the club. Dave replied by telling me that my friend who Jay wanted to talk to was also going to go. "Here are the directions to his house. We should be there around 2:30 a.m."

"Hey, we are getting ready to leave and go get something to eat, so we will see you there," I told him.

While we were waiting outside for the valet to bring us our car, I saw my sexy friend that I had met earlier in the club.

He came up to me and he asked where I was going. I told him I was on my way to an after-party.

"If you want, you can come to my house and I can give you a massage and we can relax by the fire place," he offered.

"I would love to, but I had already made plans with my friend. I might come by if it's not too late."

"I should be up. I'll call you later to see what you are doing," he said.

"Okay, call me," I replied.

My girl and I were hungry, so we got in the car and went to Jerry's Famous Deli to grab a bite to eat. When we had finished eating, we headed for Jay's house. As we turned down the street where he lived, there were a whole lot of cars parked on the street, and people were walking up to his house. By the time we walked to his house, the gate was already open. We went inside and walked past the cars and followed some girls into the kitchen. It seemed like the club was now at his house; there were people everywhere. They were in the kitchen, bedroom, and living room. There was a lot of liquor on the kitchen counter, so we made ourselves some drinks.

Lori's cell phone rang, and when she answered it, her NBA friend was asking her if she was at Jay's house yet. She told him we were already there. He said he was in the backyard playing basketball, and he wanted her to come outside where he was.

When we went outside, girls were in the Jacuzzi with their shirts off, people were in the pool swimming, and there were guys and girls playing basketball. The music was on and everyone was having a really good time.

We walked over to the basketball court where he was playing ball. He walked over to us, and gave us a hug, and asked us if we wanted to play. She and I set our drinks down, and we began to play basketball with them. We were just shooting some hoops, playing the guys against the girls.

I looked over toward the house, and I saw Jay and Dave walking over to the basketball court. They walked over to us, and started to shoot some hoops. We were all taking turns trying to see who could make the most baskets, when Jay suddenly said, "Let's play strip basketball. If you miss a shot you have to take something off."

Everyone looked at each other and said "All right, I'm down, let's play."

So Jay said, "Ladies first, who wants to start?"

"I will go first," I said.

Jay handed me the ball, and I stood at the free throw line. I bounced the ball and as soon as I began to take my shot, Jay shouted, "You're gonna miss!" I took the shot, and I made it in.

Jay called out, "Okay, you have a little skill, but it's my turn now. Watch how it should be done." The girls started talking shit; they were yelling and telling him that he wasn't gonna make it. So he said, "Okay, if yawl are so sure that I am not going to make it in, I will bet that if I do make it in, Lori has to take her shirt off."

Lori looked at him and said, "Why me, why do I have to take my shirt off? There are six other girls out here, pick one of them."

"No, that's the bet, and if I miss it I will take something off, and if I make it, you have to take off your shirt."

"Fine, but if you miss, I want you to take off your pants."

"Okay, it's a bet."

Now all the guys were yelling, "Come on Jay, you better make this. Don't make us look bad!"

Meanwhile, the girls were chanting, "Miss! Miss! Miss!" So he took the shot and not surprisingly he made it. All the guys started yelling, "Take it off! Take it off!"

Lori was laughing as she removed her shirt. Lori said, "Give me the ball, it's my turn now, damn it, and Jay will be taking off his pants."

Jay laughed. "Girl, you know you can't shoot no hoops. Stop talking shit, and just shoot the ball."

She shot the ball, and she made it. "Ha! I told you that I would make it. Now take off you pants, Jay."

Jay said, "I don't mind at all. I'm not ashamed of my nakedness." Jay began taking his pants off and the girls started whistling at him. But when he took his pants off he did not have any drawers on. All of a sudden this long dick was swinging back and forth.

The girls were like, "Where is your underwear?"

Jay laughed, "Don't be scared, just play the game. Whose turn is it?"

Everyone was laughing when one of his guy friends said, "It's my turn, give me the damn ball." So his friend took a shot and he missed.

The girls yelled, "Off with your pants!"

"All right, all right," he said. So he started doing a striptease to the music. While he was taking off his pants the girls were whistling and throwing dollar bills at him. When he removed his pants, he had on some bright red Speedos.

The guys were like, "Man, you're suppose to have on boxers, not some tight ass drawers on; you're gonna end up with a yeast infection." Everyone was clowning him; it was hilarious.

He said, "Just give one of the girls the ball, so they can take something off."

One of the girls grabbed the ball and she began to shoot it. She missed. "Off with something, take off something," the guys hollered. So she took off her skirt, and she didn't have any panties on.

Now the guys were really yelling, "Aw shit, it's on now. It's starting to get a little freaky up in here. Who is next because we need some more panties dropping?"

It was now the NBA player's turn. The girls were like, "That's not fair! You know he is going to make it. He is a professional." The guys were like, "It doesn't matter; it's the guys against the girls. Stop acting like babies and let him shoot the ball." So right when he started to shoot the ball, one of the girls began to take off her shirt. He saw her and he turned his head toward her, and he missed the shot. The guys yelled, "What are you doing man, how the hell are you going to miss the damn shot when you play in the NBA? You're off the team, get to stepping."

I said, "Hell no, he missed so he has to take something off."

Jay responded, "You just want to see his nakedness."

"You damn right," I said. "With a body like that I want to see it, so take it off."

"Its cool, how about I take it all off."

"Please do, take it off, then."

So he started taking off all his clothes, and ooh wee, did he have a nice body. His muscles were firm and cut. All the girls were yelling and staring at him. The guys were like, "I think you need to put your clothes back on, you're making us look bad out here."

The ladies didn't agree. "We are enjoying the view, leave them off."

Jay said, "Let's all go in the Jacuzzi and have some drinks."

We all grabbed our clothes and we went to the Jacuzzi. Nobody had any bathing suits, so we all decided to go skinny dipping. Everyone took off their clothes and got in the hot bubbling Jacuzzi. Jay told us he was going inside to make us some drinks. While he was gone, we were sitting in the Jacuzzi talking to each other, and looking at all the people that were in the backyard. I was starting to get really hot sitting in there, so I asked Lori if she wanted to go swimming in the pool to cool off. Lori said that she wanted to stay in the Jacuzzi until Jay got back with the drinks. About thirty minutes had gone by, when one of the girls asked, "What is taking him so long to bring the drinks out?"

One of Jay's friends said, "He probably got stopped in the kitchen while he was making them. I will go see what's going on." He left to go in the house to find him. When he came back, he told us that Jay was in the house talking to my other friend that he had met at the club, so he might be awhile before he comes back outside. "If you guys want your drinks, just go in the kitchen and make them, or I can make them and bring them out to you."

Lori said, "That's okay, we are going to get out anyway, because it is getting hot in here. Do you think he would mind if we took a shower and got dressed?"

"No, he doesn't care, I'll show you where the shower is."

We grabbed our clothes and wrapped a towel around us, and we walked into the house. He took us to the bathroom and we showered and got dressed. By the time we walked back into the kitchen to make drinks, they had started a Soul Train line. Everyone was lined up, and they were dancing down the middle of the line. Jay had a microphone and was making comments about everyone who was dancing down the line.

All of a sudden, I felt my cell phone vibrating. I picked it up and I looked at the phone number. Since I did not recognize it, I did not answer the call. One minute later, it started vibrating again. I said to my girl, "Someone is calling me from an 818 area code, and I don't recognize the phone number.

She said, "Just answer it and see who it is."

I said, "Okay, I'll be right back because I can't hear in this room." So, I went into the bathroom, and I said, "Yes."

A sexy voice said, "Is this Savannah?"

"Yes, who's speaking?"

"Don't tell me that you forgot me that fast, do I need to refresh your memory?"

"Hmm, describe yourself."

"Okay, you can see me on channel 2 every afternoon, playing Malcolm. I will be thirty years old, I also model, and all the women wanted me tonight, but I was dancing with you, enjoying your hands on my hot sweaty chest."

"Oh yeah, I remember. How could I forgot those rippling muscles, I am getting hot just thinking about it. I can't wait to touch them again."

"Why don't you come over, so you can pour some hot oil on them and rub them for me!"

"I would love to, but I have to see what my friend wants to do. Can I call you back in a minute?"

"Hurry and call me right back, because if you're not going to come over, I will have to go to bed all alone, and I know you do not want that."

"We would not want that, let me go ask her, and I will call you back in a minute."

I went back into the room, and I told her who was on the phone, and that he wanted me to go over to his house and spend the night.

Lori said, "Let me see if my friend will give me a ride home. I might stay here with him."

She went over to her NBA friend, and she told him that I was ready to go, so she had to leave. He told her if she wanted to stay, that he would take her home.

I walked over to Jay, and said, "Thank you so much for inviting me, I had a really good time, but I am getting ready to leave."

Jay asked, "What is your phone number so I can call you and invite you to the set of my show?" I gave him my phone number, and I told him to call me anytime.

As I was leaving Jay's house, I picked up my phone and called my friend back to let him know that I was on my way. He answered the phone, "So, are you coming?"

"Yeah, I'm getting in my car now."

"Good, I can't wait to see you."

"What are we going to do when I get there?"

"I am going to pour you a glass of wine, and we are going to sit by the fireplace and I am going to make love to you all night long."

"That's just what I need," I said. He gave me the directions, and I told him I should be there in twenty minutes.

As I was driving to his house, I was thinking to myself how many women watched him on television, and how they portrayed him as a sex symbol. Women would go crazy over him; they desired him. I couldn't blame them, he is fine and he does have a very, very nice body, one of the best that I have seen. He was considered to be a fantasy for many women, and I was about to find out what the reality was.

As I pulled up and parked my car, I called him on my cell phone and I told him that I was front. He said, "Come in, the door is open."

I walked up to the door, and I turned the knob, and when the door opened, he was standing there in an open, white silk shirt and white tight briefs. He had a glass of wine in his hand, and the fireplace was burning. As I turned to close the door, I felt his hand on my shoulder and he turned me around. He moved me back against the door, and he placed his left hand on the side of my face. He began to kiss me. He gently moved his tongue all around the inside of my mouth. I placed my hand on the back of his neck. We started to walk toward the fireplace as we were still kissing each other. He set the glass of wine down on the table and took his hands and placed them on my shoulders and took off my jacket. We had not stopped kissing each other yet. We kneeled down in front of the fireplace, and, as I was kissing him, I removed his shirt. I then placed my hands on his ass and gently squeezed it. It was round and firm. He then lifted my shirt from the bottom and he pulled it over my head. He laid me on my back right in front of the fireplace. He gently placed his body on top of mine, and he began to lightly move his tongue on my neck. My head was arched back, and he licked it so lightly that he made me quiver. I took my hands and I placed them in his briefs, and I started to gently move them up and down on his firm ass. I could feel his dick pressing up against my pussy. It was long and hard. He took his hands, and he pushed his upper body slightly upward. He started to move his hips around in a circle while I still had my hands on the back of his ass. He had his eyes closed and he moaned as he moved his hips on me. He quietly asked, "I want you right now, can I have you?" I nodded my head up and down.

He took his hands and placed them on my hips, and he took my white lace panties off me. Then, he took my legs and pushed them back toward my chest, and he began to lick my clit. This sexy man placed it in his mouth, and gently sucked it and licked it, at the same time. He held my legs back so I could not stop him. Finally, he lifted his head up, and he remarked, "Damn, you taste so good."

I took his arms, and I pulled him up toward me and turned him so he was lying on his back. I started to lick his chest from the top, and I kept on going until I reached his bellybutton. I started to circle it with my tongue, and, at the same time, I began to take off his boxers. I put the tip of his dick in my mouth and I began to tease it. I licked the head of it, and then I started sucking it and licked the tip again. I moved my tongue all the way down until I reached the bottom. He was moving his head and his legs back and forth on the floor moaning, and crying out, "I don't want to cum yet, I still want to make love to you. Come here."

So I stopped licking him, and began to kiss his rippling stomach all the way up to his neck. He had his arms wrapped around my waist while his hands were grabbing my ass. He rolled me over on my back, and he was now on top of me while kissing me passionately. He looked into my eyes and asked, "Are you ready for me?" I nodded.

He got the condom that was sitting on the table, and he handed it to me and he stated, "I want you to put it on me."

I opened the wrapper and I took out the condom and I placed it on the tip of his hard seven-inch dick. I held the tip of it with my left hand, while I used my other hand to slide it all the way down until I reached the base of it. He took both my hands and moved them above my head, and he held them there with one hand. He, then, moved his right hand, and put it on his dick, and he slowly inserted it inside me. His hand moved back up above my head and while he held my hands, he began to kiss my neck with his tongue. He was slowly moving his dick back and forth inside me. Then he began moving it around in circles, right on my G-Spot. He moved his dick out so that only the tip was still in me. Then he pushed it back in slowly, while squeezing his butt cheeks together, and relaxing them, back and forth. He pumped in and out while he took his hand and placed it on my cheek, putting two fingers in my mouth. I used my tongue by moving it all around his fingers as I gently sucked them. He took his fingers out and he placed them on my shoulders. He then stuck his tongue in my mouth, moving it all around. He pulled on my shoulders, while he was moving himself in and out. I took my fingers and I placed them on his back, and I started to run them up and down very lightly while his body began quivering. I moved them on his ass, and I grabbed it firmly and he started to move his hips in and out faster. He moved his dick in and out, in and out, faster and faster. Suddenly, I whispered in his ear, "I'm about to cum."

He said, "So am I, tell me when you are ready, then we can cum together." He moved himself in and out of me very fast, while he kissed me.

He pumped and pumped, hitting my G-spot. When I was ready I turned my head and said, "Now!"

He mumbled, "Okay. Here it comes." He squeezed his shoulders tight, placed his lips on mine, and moaned. I could feel his manhood inside of me pulsating, while his body trembled.

Most women have fantasized what it would be like to sleep with this gorgeous, sexy soap opera star. Was it what they have always dreamed it would be? To me, it sure was. He was very good. He was not the best I had, but good enough to go back for more. He was very caring to my needs. He made love to me, not just fucked me. He knew how to make love to me very well by the way he moved his body.

He had the type of body that women love to look at and touch. It was very well toned and spectacular. His face was sexy, his eyes seemed to pierce right through me, and his lips were a joy to kiss. My rating for him is a nine.

CHAPTER 6
Two Thumbs Down

This chapter is going to make you say, "Girl, you have got to be kidding," but I'm not. This actually did happen. Now, we have all had that one notorious date that we will never forget. The one that makes you ask yourself over and over again how you ever got into that situation in the first place, and then you laugh out loud at the thought. The one I'm about to share with you now is truly one of the ones to be remembered, and there was no way I could have guessed that the date would end up the way it did.

It was around nine o'clock on a Friday night, and I was hanging out at Tiffany's house, trying to figure out what we were going to do for the rest of the night. The club scene was burned out. We had gotten so tired of seeing the same people, singing the same old song, with the same old lines. Especially, the men trying to get some ass, simply because I let them buy me a drink. We felt like hanging out at someone's house, having a few drinks, and chilling out. It was one of those "Who can we call" kind of nights.

My girl got an idea, "Call Ray! See what he is doing tonight, maybe we can go over there, and I can finally hook up with him."

"That sounds like a good idea. Hand me your phone, so I can call him," I said. I immediately dialed his number. Ray answered promptly, "Hey, what's going tonight?" I asked eagerly.

"I'm with my boy Bobby right now at my house. We are getting ready to go to the hotel to hang out with his wife and my sister. Who are you with?"

"My girl Tiffany. We are trying to find something to do tonight. Can we hang out with you?"

"Well, what does your friend look like?" he said.

"She's about 5'4," blonde hair, big boobs, and she has a nice shape. You will like her. If you aren't busy, I could bring her by, and you can see for yourself."

"You can come hang out with us, come to the house right now, and you can follow us to the hotel," Ray suggested.

"Okay we are on our way."

I hung up the phone and told Tiffany, "Ray wants to meet you, and he said we can hang out with him tonight, but we need to leave now because he is about to leave and go to some hotel."

She was definitely Ray's type, so I knew he wouldn't be disappointed. He and I had hung out before in the past and he always knew where to go to have a good time. Any night of the week he knew where the excitement was.

We arrived at the gate, and I told the guard that we were here to see Ray. When he lets us in, we parked the car in front of his condo and walked up to the front door. We rang the bell, and we stood there for a minute, but no one answered. "Maybe they left," Tiff said.

"He wouldn't leave and not call me; that's not really like him. Ring it again."

Finally, Ray answered the door. He had a drink in his hand. His black cap was turned backward, and he had on a big beige sweater and blue jeans. He looked kind of faded. Ray gave us a hug. As I introduced Tiffany, I could tell by the look on his face that he liked the way she looked. When we walked inside, he gave my friend a tour of the downstairs area since that was her first time being there.

When you are at the door and you look straight ahead, there are stairs that lead you to the second floor. When you turn to the left and walk a few feet you enter the dining room area. To the right of the dining room, is a modern-looking kitchen, with wood cabinets. When you walk out of the kitchen, and go straight, you would walk down a few stairs to enter the living room.

While we were in the living room, Ray told us to have a seat and asked us if we wanted anything to drink. "Sure," I said, "Make us the same thing you are drinking."

He made us some vodka and cranberry juice. When he handed us our drinks he said, "I'll be right back, I'm going to go upstairs and get my boy."

After he left the room, I immediately said to my girl, "So, what do you think about Ray? Do you still want to hook up with him?"

"Hell, yeah!"

"I'll find out what's up when he comes back downstairs. I wonder who his boy is that is up there. I guess we will find out soon enough."

About fifteen minutes went by and we had not heard a word. We looked at each other, wondering what he was doing up there. Right then, he came down, and right behind him was his boy, with a cigarette and a drink in his hand. I knew who he was; I grew up listening to the six-member East Coast group he used to sing in. He looked thuggish. He was dressed casually, in all black. He stood about six feet tall, with short black hair, and his lips slightly poked out with a gap between his teeth. As Ray introduced Bobby to us, he looked at my girl and I, and said, "Damn, what's going on ladies, yawls are looking real good."

"Not too much, just waiting on you to keep us company," I said.

"Sorry to keep you ladies waiting, can I make you another drink?"

"No thanks, we're okay."

"Then if we're all done drinking, let's go," Ray said.

They got into his silver Mercedes, and we got in our car and followed them to the hotel. When we got to the Le Meridian Hotel, Ray called me on my cell phone and said, "Savannah, let us go in first, and then you guys come in to the lounge in about ten minutes, so his girl won't start tripping."

"That's fine, I understand, I will see you in a few." We turned the radio up and touched up our makeup and hair.

"Should we go in there, now?" Tiff asked.

"It's been long enough. Let's go in."

As we walked to the lobby, I told my girl, "Let's just go to the bar and get some drinks and don't even look their way, so we don't get him in trouble."

"You have a good point, I am not trying to have any drama tonight." When we reached the lounge, we saw Ray and Bobby, who was now with his wife, and a few other people sitting at their table. They were all just talking and having some drinks. We walked right past them and didn't say anything. Tiffany and I didn't even look at them. We went straight to the bar and ordered our drinks.

While we were waiting, Bobby walked up to the bar, about five feet from where we were standing, and ordered a drink. He did not look at us at all. All of a sudden, Ray walked up to us with Bobby's diva wife. He told her our names, and we shook hands. As she introduced herself, she shook our hands rapidly and spoke just as fast, like she was on something. We both said "It's nice to meet you." The bartender interrupted, and we turned to grab our drinks. By the time we turned back to face her, she had already gone back to her table, so my girl and I proceeded to walk to our table, nowhere near theirs.

We sat down and as were talking, Ray came up to us and said, "You guys are going to have to leave."

I asked him why, and he said, "His girl thinks that you were trying to talk to him."

"What, are you serious?" I exclaimed.

"Yeah, just go, he and I will call you when we are leaving," he said.

"But I didn't even look at him. Is she that insecure? Some diva she is."

"I'm sorry, but I don't want her to cause a scene. So just go, and we will call. I promise."

"So, what are we going to do until they call?" My girl asked.

"I know, call Suave and see what clubs are happening tonight. You know he has lots of connections since he is a porn star. He'll know where we can go and kill some time."

We called, and Suave told us about a club on Third Street that he was at.

"Do you want to go?" I asked Tiff.

"Yeah, what else are we going to do? If we go home I'll end up falling asleep, so let's just go make the best of it until they call us back."

We arrived at the club around eleven o'clock. There was a line to get in, but we walked straight to the front, and security let us right in since he knew who we were. It was a good size crowd, and the atmosphere was pretty mellow. We went to the bar and ordered drinks (since we didn't get to finish the last one because of that crazy situation at the hotel). We began walking around trying to find a table. We managed to find Suave, so we sat down with him and told him about the hotel story. He was laughing so hard he could hardly even believe it!

About an hour went by before my cell phone rang. "Hello!"

"Where are you guys?" Ray asked.

"The club on Third Street," I told him. "Where are you?"

"We are just leaving the hotel. Meet us in the parking lot right now."

"All right, we are on our way." I told Tiff, "They want us to go back to meet them, so put the cigarette out and let's bounce."

When we got to the hotel, we parked and then walked over to Ray's car. Bobby was in the driver's seat, and Ray was in the passenger seat. As soon as we got to them, Ray yelled, "Get in, get in!" He was laughing. We opened the door and got in the backseat, and Ray's boy sped off like a bat out of hell!

"What the hell is going on?" I asked.

Bobby replied, "My girl and his sister just got in their car, and we have got to get out of here before she sees us. If she sees you two in the backseat, she is going to go off. You don't understand, my girl is crazy!"

"Yeah, I noticed that!" I said.

He slammed his foot on the gas pedal fast. The tires screeched, and we sped off down the street, like we were in NASCAR races. He looked in his rear view mirror and yelled, "Shit, here they come! I have gotta lose um!" He started darting in and out of traffic, driving like a maniac, almost hitting cars. We approached the intersection as the light turned red. I assumed that he was going to stop at the light, but he was not slowing down.

My girl yelled, "Stop, the light is red; what the hell are you doing!"

He yelled back, "I have to run it, or she will see you in the car. Hold on!" He ran the red light, and the oncoming traffic slammed on their brakes to avoid hitting us. People were honking their horns and yelling. Suddenly, he made a quick right turn down a residential street losing control of the car! The car turned left, and then right, it was shaking back and forth.

My friend and I were screaming, "We're going to crash! Slow down!" Sure enough, the right side of the car clipped a tree, and our two obviously unstable companions began laughing hysterically as they stumbled from the car. I looked over at my friend and I said to her, "Well, I'm sober now! This damn fool is crazy, is he for real? Oh hell no, we gotta get out of here."

We got out of the car to look at the damage. "It's not that bad, the front light is broken and the fender is a little dented," Ray said.

When we got back in the car, I pleaded, "Please let Ray drive, so I can live to see another day."

Bobby said, "Sorry, man, I didn't mean for that to happen." He took off his diamond ring and handed it to Ray, "Here take this for the damage to the car."

"It's cool," Ray said as he put the ring on. "Don't worry about it."

"At least we lost them. Are you guys cool in the back?" Ray's boy asked?

"Yeah, let's get out of here, before we all go to jail for DUI and God knows whatever else. The cops in this neighborhood will probably think we kidnapped this white girl," I said laughingly. "Just kidding, let's go."

"Where are we going?" Tiff asked.

"Let's just go to my house," Ray said.

When we got back to his house, we all were so tired from the car chase that we just sat on the couch and started watching a movie. I sat down on the left end of the couch, and my girl sat on the other end. Ray went upstairs to change his clothes and to check his messages. Bobby went into the kitchen to make us some drinks. When he came back into the living room, he ended up sitting next to me. When Ray came back downstairs, he sat next to my girl and started talking with her. About halfway through the movie, Ray said, "Let's go upstairs."

We went into Ray's room, and all four of us laid across the bed. Nobody was saying anything, so I spoke up. "It's too quiet in here, turn on some music."

"I have something better than that," Bobby said. He got up and started singing and doing his old school dances that he did when he sang with his group. Then Ray joined in, and started singing and dancing also. It was hilarious. We just watched them as they put on a show. All of a sudden Bobby grabs my hand and pulls me off the bed and takes me into another bedroom.

The room was dark inside. The window was open and the light from the moon was shining on us. He put his arm around me and stuck his tongue down my throat. He was kissing me so forcefully, that I felt like I was about to gag. His lips were totally covering my mouth as if he was trying to swallow my face! I turned my head so he would stop kissing me.

Then, he moved his mouth toward my neck and he put his tongue on it. He began licking it very aggressively. While he was kissing and licking my neck, I wiped his spit off my mouth; it was disgusting. It smelled like old alcohol. I wanted him to stop, so I started to unbutton his pants. I could not get the button undone, so he undid it himself. He grabbed my hand and put it in his pants. He told me to squeeze it. So I squeezed gently, and he said, "No harder, squeeze it really hard…now stroke it up and down on the head."

"Like this, baby?" I said.

"Oh, yeah, that's how I like it…just like that." He put his hands behind his head, lacing his fingers together. He watched me stroke it up and down hard and fast. His hips were going back and forth. "Shit, baby, I need to stick it in you now!" He moaned.

So I laid my hand on his chest and pushed gently, leaning him down to the floor. I grabbed his hands and put them above his head. My legs were wrapped around his waist.

While holding his hands above his head, I kissed his neck really lightly, and then I licked his neck. It tasted like salt and sweat, as if he had just run a marathon. Between the salty taste in my mouth and the smell of alcohol, I thought I was taking a shot of tequila. "Ewe," I thought. If his neck tastes like that, I could imagine what it would taste like if I went down on him. So I decided, I don't think so. Savannah don't play that.

Ray always had condoms in the nightstands, so I opened the drawer, and I grabbed a condom out of it. I ripped it open with my teeth and put the condom on his seven-inch penis. It was just an average size, dark, with a small head. I put it inside me and began to ride him, back and forth, and then in circles. He put his hands on my ass, and squeezed it firmly. I could see the motion of his head moving from side to side as he grunted and moaned. Next, I rode him really fast, moving my hips up and down so quickly that it started to make a clapping sound. About twenty minutes had gone by, and all of a sudden I saw his arm reach up toward the table next to us. He grabbed a glass and threw it against the wall. It shattered everywhere!

"What's wrong?" I whispered.

He said, "I'm about to cum."

Thank God, I thought, because this was whack! He grunted again, squeezed my arms, and do you believe this fool started singing while he was having an orgasm? I did not say a thing. I was trying to hold in my laughter. I got off him and walked to the bathroom carefully, so I wouldn't step on the glass on the floor. Despite my caution, I did anyway. I felt the pain of the glass in my foot, but all I could do was laugh. I mean, after all that I had experienced that night, I just had to laugh. I took a shower, cleaned my foot, and headed back to the bedroom. I turned on the light in the room so I could find my clothes, and I saw him passed out on the floor in the same position that I left him. Now, was that a night or what!

This celebrity, I'll have to give two thumbs down. He was a mess, his kissing was way too sloppy. He did absolutely nothing to turn me on, and the sex was just booty. To make it even worse, he could have killed us in the car. This singer deserves a negative two rating. I know that is bad, but I am just keeping it real.

CHAPTER 7
The Fetish

There was a famous R&B singer who had a major foot fetish addiction, which was out of control. Every time we were intimate together, he would always be looking at my feet damn near the whole time. When he would call me to come over and see him, he would always say, "Make sure that you are wearing pink nail polish on your toes, and make sure the shoes you are wearing are open so that I can see them."

One time when I went over to his place, I was not wearing open-toed shoes, and he got upset and wanted me to go change them. After that, every single time before I would go and see him, he would call me on the phone to say, "Make sure that you are wearing the shoes that I like."

The next time that I came over to visit him, he sat me down in a chair, took off my right high heeled shoe, and then he opened a blue velvet jewelry box. He took out a diamond toe ring, and he placed it on my second toe. He began to massage my toe, for about two minutes and then he would move on to the next one rubbing it gently. After he finished massaging all my toes, he would take his hands all the way down to my ankle and massage it for a few minutes. He would then move his hands up and down my entire foot vigorously; it felt so good. His hands were big and strong that when he took my foot in his hands and rubbed it, it felt like all the stress that I had in my body, was being released through my feet. He knew how to give the best foot massages that I have ever experienced. It felt like he had taken a class on how to be a professional massage therapist. He knew the anatomy of the foot well, and he would rub all the pressure points perfectly. When he did rub my feet, he would take his knuckles, and move them in a circular motion on the bottom of my foot. He then would take his hands and rub the sides of my foot while rubbing my ankles. If his singing career ever ends, he could definitely have a future in giving foot massages.

One day when we were having lunch together, we decided to go back to his place to relax before we went to his concert. While I was lying on the bed trying to take a nap, he said to me, "Give me a foot massage." He was lying on the bed with his shoes still on. I took off his shoes and socks, and I began to rub both his feet at the same time. I used my hands to rub the top of his feet from side to side. I began to move my hands under the bottom of his feet, and I started to lightly run my finger tips over them. He started to moan and pulled his feet away from me. I looked up at him, and he was taking off his pants and underwear. I took a hold of his clothes and pulled them off his legs. He said, "Keep running your fingers on the bottom of my feet, it feels so good." I again started moving my fingers along the bottom of his feet. He flinched them and sighed while I was doing it. I took one of his feet, and I placed his toes in my mouth. My tongue was moving on the bottom of his toes in a circular motion, and then I would move it between them. I started to gently suck them one by one. He took his foot away from my tongue, and he told me to rub his right foot up and down, as fast as I could with some baby oil on it. I took the baby oil, and I tipped it upside down, and I let it run all down his foot. I put the oil back on the nightstand, and I placed my hand on his toes, and I began to slowly rub the oil into his foot. I took my hand and moved it up and down as fast as I could, from his ankles to his toes. I stroked it up and down, for about four minutes. He watched me stroke his feet, while his manhood was hard as a rock. He murmured, "Faster, stroke it faster."

I moved my hand faster on his foot. Then, he said, "Just like that, don't stop, I'm about to cum!" I kept on moving at that pace, and the next thing I knew the semen from his manhood squirted all over his chest. Wow, neither of us even touched his manhood at all. He had an orgasm, just by me stroking his foot. Now tell me that this man does not have a mad crazy foot fetish.

Here is another episode, which I found quite bizarre. I was lying on my stomach, in my bra and panties reading a magazine. My feet were slightly hanging off the edge of the bed. He had just gotten out of the shower, and he had a towel wrapped around his waist. I saw him walk behind me, but I was not paying attention to what he was doing. All of a sudden, I feel him pick up my foot and put his dick on the bottom of it. He started to move his dick back and forth on the bottom of my foot. His right hand held down the top of it, while the bottom of it rubbed back and forth on my foot. His left hand was around my ankle, holding it up against his body, under his dick. I turned around, and I said to him, "What are you doing?"

He said, "I want to cum on your feet." So I turned back around, and I kept on reading my magazine while he got his rocks off. He basically was fucking my foot. He was moving his hips back and forth on my foot until he climaxed.

I have to tell you just one more situation. We had just gotten back from a movie premiere. It was late at night so we decided to take a shower and go to bed. When I got out of the shower I was feeling hot and horny, so I decided that I was going to give him a strip show. I turned on some music, and I told him to sit down in the chair. I slowly walked over to him, I turned around, and I bent over in front of him and touched my toes. I shook my ass cheeks one at a time right in front of his face. I bent my knees, and dropped my ass all the way to the floor. I placed my hands on my knees, and I pushed them open and then closed them, so he could see between my legs. I sat on the floor, and I began to put my feet in the air pointing my toes. I was moving my legs in different ways, opening and closing them. I looked at his eyes, and the whole time that I was dancing, he was only looking at my damn feet. He never looked at my tits or my secret garden, just my feet. So I thought to myself, what should I do to get him to look at something other than my feet? I decided to take my finger and put it inside my sugar walls, and rub it all on the inside of my lips. It still did not work; he continued looking at my feet.

I got up from the floor, and sat on his lap. I wrapped my legs around him so he could not look at my feet. He immediately looked at me. I grabbed the back of the chair with my hands, and I started shaking my breasts in his face. While I was giving him a lap dance, he took his hands, and he placed them on my hips, he was watching them move around his lap. I place my hands on the back of his head, and I began to kiss him gently. He wrapped his arms around my waist, and he picked me up and carried me to the bed. He laid me down on my back with my legs still wrapped around his waist, kissing me on my neck. I was ready for his nine inches to go deep inside me, so I took a condom from the nightstand, and I gave it to him. He pushed his hard, thick manhood inside me, and he began to fuck me real slow. He told me to point my toes. While he was on top of me, pumping in and out, his head was turned to the side looking at my feet. He would turn and look at me for a second, but then he would turn back and look at my feet again. Ten minutes had gone by, and we were still in the same position. He took my legs and moved them all the way to my chest, so that my knees were bent and my feet were on his chest. He told me to take my feet and push on his chest. So I pushed my feet on his chest, while he was rapidly pumping in and out of me. "Now grab your feet and hold them," he moaned.

I took hold of my feet, and he pulled his manhood out of me, pulled the condom off, and he came all over my feet.

While we were lying in bed, I decided that I was going to ask him why he had such a fetish for feet. I just had to know what really fascinated him about feet. I was trying to decide on how I should bring it up. Fuck it, I should just come out and ask it. So I sat on top of him, and I said, "Why do you have such a fetish for my feet?"

He laughed and said, "It's a long story."

I said, "Tell me, I really want to know."

He replied, "Okay, it started when I was about eleven years old, my mom worked as a manicurist, and I would often go to work with her. The women would always have their shoes off, and I would always look at them. I would watch my mom paint their toes, and massage their feet. I would watch them get their toes painted pink. So ever since, I have always had a thing for pretty feet. They just turn me on. Don't get me wrong, I still love other parts of a woman's body, but I am fascinated by a woman's feet. Especially if a woman has beautiful feet, which are well manicured with pink polish, I am turned on by them."

Well, there you have it. Is this a good reason to have such an addictive fetish? I don't know, you decide. I am going to put this chapter to sleep!

Let me describe my foot fetish singer. My medium brown singer, is a songwriter, and a record producer. He is very tall, with a nice build, and he has lots of tattoos on his arms and chest. He has no hair, but he usually wears a mustache and beard. His face is average, and he has big lips. He always has a pair of sunglasses on, and he is grown and sexy. That's enough clues or I will give it away too easily.

I am going to give him a six; the whole situation was just average. He kisses just average, not enough to turn me on. Besides, it was the foot massages that were great. The sex was a little strange; I never had someone so fascinated with feet before. His looks were all right, nothing special, but he did treat me pretty good, and I had fun when I was with him. Maybe if he was into other parts of me, besides my feet, he might receive a better rating.

CHAPTER 8
Mr. Mandingo

This celebrity that I was partially intimate with one time, and I say partially because his manhood was so big...no, huge...that it would only fit partially inside me. So, that one time was plenty.

I'll describe him so you can have an idea of what he looks like. He is very tall; I would say he is about 6'11." He has a medium build structure, but he does not have rippling muscles, just average, with a nice firm tone. He has no hair, but his head is well groomed so it is nice and smooth when you touch it. It reminds me of a milk dud...smooth, shiny, and dark. His face is average looking, but when he smiles, it makes him look cute. His skin is a medium-toned complexion. His lips are nice and full. He usually wears a goatee. He is a nice looking man, not fine, but he is cute enough to make you take a second look. I would give him a seven on looks. He played both power forward and center for the Detroit Pistons, is an actor and sports talk show host, also. I refer to him as Mr. Mandingo throughout this chapter. But enough with that, let's get to the good stuff.

A good friend of mine, Herb, was one of the hottest club promoters in Los Angeles, and had all the connections in the entertainment industry. If there was a hot party going on in Los Angeles, he was always there. Almost every night he was at the clubs networking. He came in contact with many celebrities with whom he became friends. Herb knew what clubs were happening on any given night. If I needed to get on the VIP list, all I had to do is just call him, and I was on the list. He had access to the top of the line mansion parties, celebrities' phone numbers, and complete VIP treatment. He was the man to call if I wanted to attend an event that was full of celebrities.

He called me one night just to say hi and to see what I was doing. I wasn't up to much of anything, my girl Ann and I were watching television and hanging out. Herb invited me on the set of his friend's television talk show.

"If you want to come, you need to leave now, because the show is going to start soon."

"Can I bring my girl with me?"

He said, "It depends on who you are bringing, you can't bring her if she is ugly."

"I don't roll with ugly friends, all my girls are dime pieces, and you know that."

"I know, I'm just kidding. Make sure that you two are here soon and call me when you get to the parking lot, so I can meet you at the door and take you backstage. I want you to meet my boy who hosts the show, so remind me to introduce you to him."

"Okay, we will be there in about thirty minutes, and I will hit you on your cell when I get to the parking lot."

Ann and I were fine with what we were wearing. She had on a short black skirt with black high heals and a blue shirt that fit tightly. Her brown hair was pulled back into a curly ponytail. I was wearing a pair of tight jeans and a low cut shirt. My hair was straight and down. We were not dressed up at all, but still looked good. All we had to do was touch up our makeup. We left the house and we headed for the studio. Ann wanted to stop at the store to buy some alcohol, to make the night more interesting.

When we arrived in the parking lot of the studio where the show was, I called Herb. As soon as he got to the car, he noticed Ann was having a drink. He said to her, "Is that drink drink?"

She said, "Yeah, do you want some?"

"Hell, yeah, let me in so I can get my drink on." He got in the backseat and he ended up having a quick drink with her before he took us inside the studio.

As we walked into the huge warehouse with tall, gray, stone walls, there were thick, long, different colored wires all over the floor. We had to walk over and around them. Men and women were working everywhere, throwing and gathering wires, and sitting behind huge black cameras.

There were additional walls throughout the warehouse that separated different areas of the set. One area had a table laid out with refreshments and food. Another had big boxes and stage equipment, and then there was the stage and audience section. We walked along the perimeter of the warehouse and finally reached the dressing rooms.

The dressing room was designed to look like it was outside, like a cottage. It had windows with curtains, and the door was very tall. His name was on the door in gold letters. When we walked inside, the room smelled so good, like the cologne he was wearing. He had everything in that room, all the necessary provisions—a bar, televisions, bathroom with shower. It was very nice. There was a huge fur rug in the middle of the floor in front of the television. I was tempted to lie on it; it looked so soft and comfortable. There was a couch and two recliner chairs. I took one and Ann took the other. Herb walked over and started talking to Mr. Mandingo.

There was a knock at the door and a short, blonde woman came in and began putting on his makeup. Then another knock and someone came in and said, "On in fifteen minutes."

After that, Herb walked over to us and said, "Let me introduce you to him before he has to leave and start the show."

He took us over to him and introduced us. Mr. Mandingo thanked us for coming to the show and asked if we'd come backstage afterwards so he could talk to us some more. I told him that we would be here when it was over, and it was nice meeting him. He turned to Herb and told him to take us to our seats. By the time we were seated in the audience, the show was just about to begin. He had the Wu-Tang Clan and Shaggy as his guests. Mr. Mandingo was a good host. He was very funny and he kept the audience entertained.

After the show was over, we went backstage to hang out. Ann and I were talking and eating some of the food that was on the table. I turned around and I could see he was looking over at us while he was talking to Method Man, so I smiled at him. They walked up to us and Mr. Mandingo introduced us to Method Man. Method gave us a hug and said, "What's up."

That man is oh so fine! I really enjoyed talking to him.

During our conversation Mr. Mandingo asked me, "Can I talk to you alone?"

"Sure." I told my friend that I would be back in a minute.

As we were walking away, he asked me if I enjoyed the show. I told him we had a good time, and I would love to come back again. He said, "Anytime, take down my number and call me when you want to come back. Can I get your phone number so I can take you out sometime?"

"That sounds good, just give me a call, and we can set up a date," I said.

"I will give you a call this weekend." He gave me a hug and my friend and I left the set.

Sure enough, Mr. Mandingo called me on Friday night and asked me what I was doing. I told him I was at home with my friend watching TV. He said he was in his car and asked where I lived so he could stop by. I gave him the directions, but I told him to give us an hour so we could get ready.

I hung up and told Kristen who I was talking to on the phone and that he was on his way over. She told me that she'd heard a rumor that he had a really big dick.

I said, "Are you serious, how big?"

"Ahh, rumor has it that it is huge, and he calls it the "Spider." I dare you to ask him if it is true."

"All right, when he gets here, I will ask him and we will find out if it's true." By the time we finished getting the house and ourselves ready, an hour had gone by before the doorbell finally rang.

When I opened the door, I was overwhelmed by the aroma of the cologne he had on. It reminded me of his dressing room. It smelled light and fresh, like he had just gotten out of the shower. He was wearing a long, silk, white shirt, light-colored jeans, and Jordan tennis shoes.

He came into the house, and I introduced him to my friend. He smiled and shook her hand. We showed him around the house, and while he was walking through it, his head almost touched the ceiling. I told him to have a seat on the couch, and I asked him if he wanted anything to drink or eat.

He said, "No, I just had dinner, but you can turn the television on so I can watch the basketball game." While we were watching the game, my friend kept giving me this look like I should ask him.

I finally whispered to her, "I will, hold on."

During half time, we were all talking, when I said to him, "Do you mind if I ask you a personal question?"

"No, what's the question?"

"I heard you have a really big tallywhacker?"

He smiled and said, "Yeah, how did you hear about it?"

I replied, "I heard about it from a friend of mine, is it really that big?"

He said, "Do you want to see it?"

I looked at my friend, and I said, "What do you think?"

My friend said, "Oh yeah, I have to see if the rumors are true."

So he said, "All right, but don't be scared." He unbuttoned his pants and pulled the zipper down and took it out.

My friend's eyes opened wide and her mouth dropped open, too. I said, "Holy shit, you've got to be fucking kidding me, that shit is humongous." The scary thing about it was that it wasn't even hard. I looked at my friend and she still had her mouth open while staring at it. She could not take her eyes off it.

It was about thirteen inches long, maybe even bigger than that, and about six inches in width around, with a big ass head on it. I said to him, "There is no way that anaconda would fit inside of anybody!"

He said, "I know, most girls look at it and they will not have sex with me, because they are scared of it. Why, do you two want to try it?"

I looked at my friend and she looked at me, with her mouth still open, and I said to her, "What do you think?"

She said, "Yeah, I'm down, but I don't think that it's going to fit, but we can try."

We went into the bedroom and we started taking off our clothes. My friend and I lay on our backs on the bed with our knees bent while he put on a condom that only covered a little bit pass the head. He started with me, first. As he began to put it inside me, I grabbed my friend's hand, and I squeezed it tightly hoping he would not rip me in two, with me ending up having an "Assgina." He gently pushed it in, but the only thing that was fitting was the head. Now, that was just plain ridiculous. He then moved his hips around in a circular motion, and, at the same time, he was trying to push it further inside me. I could feel my pussy getting really full. It felt like I'd stuck a whole bunch of apples in my mouth until no more could fit, but I pushed that last one in and my lips started to crack and burn. This is how it basically felt. It felt full like it was being stretched as far as it would go. He was stretching it as if he was preparing me to have a baby. The pain, the pain felt like it was splitting and scorching. I turned my head and looked at my friend, and I started to give her these looks and making faces at her, like, girl, this shit hurts and I can't take it anymore! I had taken it long enough, which was only about five minutes. I told him that he needed to stop, but before he took it out, I wanted to see how much he had managed to get in. I leaned forward to look at it. Do you know he only had three inches inside me! Yes, that was it. Is that crazy or what? Now can you understand how long and thick it was. Basically, only just his head and a little bit more fit. Oh, yeah, I almost forgot his balls. They were big, too. They were about twice the size of an average man. They hung low and had a lot of skin around them. I told him, "This is just not going to work for me, so get up and take it out, and maybe she can handle the anaconda."

He started laughing and she said, "Let me try, it's my turn."

I said, "With pleasure, because he is not gonna stretch me all out, good luck."

He took off our condom, which had to have been a super magnum or special made, because there is no way a regular one would fit. But then again, the condom barley fit on him.

While he was putting on a new one, I told my friend, "I hope you are ready for this. There is no way that it is going to fit."

She said, "Probably not, but I have to try it."

"Don't say that I didn't warn you."

He had the condom on, and he lay on top of my friend while telling her, "I know you can handle it, just relax."

He tried to put the anaconda in her, and she yelled, "That is enough, I'm cool, you're gonna give me a hysterectomy."

He said, "Damn, I barely even put it in, are you sure you ain't no virgin, girl?"

She said, "As big as that thing is, I feel like it is my first time."

"I told you, I told you," I said.

He got off her and he said, "I'm not gonna leave you disappointed, lay back and I will take care of the two of you." So, we lay back, but we were both kind of hesitant. He took his hands and gently opened my legs. He took his tongue and placed it on my inner thigh and began to run it all the way up until he reached my opening and slid his tongue all the way in until he reached my clit. His tongue moved up and down fast. He never took his tongue off it. He just kept moving it up and down, up and down, until I climaxed. When I climaxed, I grabbed the pillow, squeezing it tight, and I began to yell in it. My body was shaking and I was going crazy. He was still licking me even after I had climaxed, I took my hand and pushed his head down.

"Enough, shit, it's too sensitive right now; take care of my girl, she's ready."

So I got up and went in the shower while he took care of her. I felt kind of bad that we got ours, and he did not get his. I don't mind hooking a brother up, but I knew that if it didn't fit inside me, there was no way it was going to fit in my mouth. I was not even about to try it, damn that. He's a celebrity; he will find somebody that can handle it. He'll be all right.

It is hard for me to rate the sexual experience with him, because his tally whacker was so ridiculously big it barely fit inside me, so I can't tell you how he works it. He's cool to hang out with, and his looks are decent. I will, though, give him two thumbs up for knowing how to work his tongue very well. Since he did make me cum, I will give him a seven. If you think you can handle him, then, I would recommend it. But I seriously doubt you can!

CHAPTER 9
Marathon Man

This celebrity would keep going and going and going. When we use to have sex, we would be doing it for hours before he would climax. One hour would go by, then two, three, and before I knew it, we would be going on five hours and he still had not climaxed yet. I enjoyed having sex with him, but by the time we finished, I was exhausted.

One night he called to invite Trish and I to a party he was having at his mansion. He also mentioned that he wanted me to spend the night. So I packed up my overnight bag, and we headed for his house. During the night, he had an unexpected female that showed up. I saw him go upstairs with her, but I did not say anything about it. All I know, is it was around 2:00 a.m. and I was tired and ready to go. Trish and I decided to leave and go home. We were almost home, and my cell phone rings. I saw the number, I knew who it was, so I picked it up.

"Yeah."

"Why did you leave?"

"You had company, so I did not want to bother you, so I left."

"It was not even like that, come back to the house."

"Hold on a minute." I set the phone down on my lap, and I asked my girl if she wanted to go back to the house. She did not mind going back, so we turned around and went back.

When we got there, everyone had left, so it was just him and the two of us. As we walked in the house, he grabbed me and started to kiss me so intense, that my knees almost buckled.

Trish said "What about me?"

He looked at me, and said, "I will not sleep with her if you do not want me to, so it is up to you."

"I really don't want to share you, but if this is what you want, then so be it."

We went to the living room, and he started to take off my clothes, and I was taking off his. He started with me first. He was fucking me and fucking me for about an hour when I said to him, "Go and take care of Trish."

He got up off me and went over to her. I was watching Television while they were getting busy. I swear to you, about an hour went by, and he still did not bust a nut. She looked over at me, and said "Oh no, my pussy is raw, you take over, this is too much for me."

She got up, and I went back over to him. We had sex for about two more hours, and he still, had no orgasm yet. I told Trish, "It's your turn again, come take over." She looked at me as if I was crazy.

"Are you serious, all right, but if Mr. Marathon Man does not bust one soon, I am done, he is killing me."

Another hour went by, and still nothing. She got up off him and said "Oh hell no, this is enough, you should have busted one already. I don't know what else to do, let's go." She grabbed her stuff and told me to come on. I gave him a kiss and we left.

Mr. Marathon Man always took a long time to climax. I really don't know why he takes so long. Most women would love to have a man that can last and last, but after a while, I was ready for him to climax. It was a good work out, but my legs would get cramps in them.

Not only was the sex good, but I really liked to hang out with him. When I would go visit him at the W Hotel, I would have so much fun. We would play video games; listen to some music, and blaze one. We would then watch some television and talk about what was going on in the world.

After a few hours of relaxing, I would start to look at his lips, and I could not wait to kiss them. He had the type of lips that were so juicy. I could not wait for him to place them on mine. I just wanted to kiss them over and over again. When he finally did kiss me, he would place his hand on the side of my face so gently. We would kiss for a long time passionately, and I would not want him to stop. His tongue was so soft, and he would move it perfectly. Damn the sex, the kissing and just being around him, was good enough.

Let me describe him to you. He is a rapper and an actor. He is about 6ft tall, and has a caramel color complexion. He was born in Newark, New Jersey. He usually wears a goatee, and a light beard. He has dark brown eyes and nice lips. He was with Def Jam Records, and he loves to blaze. He also has his own clothing line.

Mr. Marathon Man was one of the most down to earth people that I knew. He had a very good personality, and he was fine as a mother. Besides the sex being long, it was still very good. I loved being around him. I will give him a nine.

CHAPTER 10
Can't Get it Up

This was one situation, in which I would never want to be in again as long as I live. There was this one celebrity singer who was a sad case in bed, but there was a reason behind it. He used drugs, and I am not talking about weed or ecstasy, I am talking about crack cocaine. Yes, crack. He used so much of it that he could not get it up, when it was time to perform.

It was mind boggling to me that such a talented man was hooked on crack-cocaine. What would make a person, who has all the money in the world, and whose career was doing very well, want to do such a harmful drug? I cannot answer that question because I never did ask him why he was using it. The trip thing about it was that he was so open with it. He never did try to hide it; he sat in front of me and did it like it was the thing to do. You would think because he was in the public eye that he would not want anyone to know that he was using crack. Not him. He did not even care that I knew. Let's get to the story.

I met him at the gym, when I was working out with my trainer. I was doing some leg weights, and my trainer said, "Here comes a good friend of mine." He walked up to him, and he started talking. He asked if he could work out with us. My trainer said, "Yeah that's cool, if it is okay with Savannah."

I looked at him, and I said, "It's fine with me, if you can keep up."

Mr. Limp smiled, and he said, "If I can't, can you teach me how?" My trainer then introduced us, and we started working out together.

During our workout, he mentioned that he was in town for a few weeks to perform at a concert, and he would like me to go. I asked, "When is it?"

He said, "Tonight."

I answered, "I wish I could, but I already have plans tonight. Can we set something up for another time?" He gave me his phone number, and he told me to call him when I was not busy.

I would have gone, but I did have plans to go see "Daddy," and there was no way that I could call him and cancel our date. "Daddy" would have been pissed off if I had tried that. He was spoiled and did not take no for an answer.

I ended up calling Mr. Limp, a few days later, to see if he wanted some company for the evening. He told me his schedule was free, and if I wanted to come over I could. I took down the directions, and I told him I would be there in a couple of hours.

When I got to the hotel, I walked to the front desk and I advised the female who was working behind the counter whom I was there to see. She raised her eyebrow, and looked at me funny like, "Who are you, and why are you here to see him?" I paid her no attention, as I stood there watching her dial his room number.

The female clerk said to him, "Are you expecting someone? You have a guest down here who says you are." She hung the phone up, and said, "He's in room #1101. Here is the elevator key. Go to the eleventh floor and go to your right."

I walked to the elevator, inserted the card, and pushed number eleven. When I got to the eleventh floor and made a right, I could see a guard standing outside a door toward the end of the hall. He was wearing a black suit, a white-collar shirt, and a red bowtie. He was staring directly at my eyes, as I walked toward him. I thought to myself, "That must be his room, but does he really need a bodyguard outside the door?"

As I got closer to the door, I could see the room number next to the guard. That was his suite. I walked up to the guard, and before I could say anything, he inquired, "What's your name?"

"Savannah," I said.

He opened the door for me and said, "Go straight and make a left. He is in the first door on the right."

I began walking down the slightly lit hallway, and I suddenly smelled something weird. It reminded me of the smell of Christmas trees, the pine odor. The closer I got to the door, the stronger it smelled. The door was closed so I knocked on it. No one answered. I knocked again, and I could faintly hear him mumble, "Come in."

I turned the knob and opened the door. I looked to the right, and he was sitting up in the bed leaning back against the headboard. He did not have any clothes on, and the white bed sheet was covering him up to his waist. This famous celebrity was holding his head with both hands. He had a real confused look on his face, almost like he was in another world. I looked down on the nightstand, and I saw a clear glass pipe, a lighter, and a solid rock-shaped substance on it. I could not believe my eyes. Here was a very famous, talented person doing crack.

I looked at him and I said, "Are you all right?"

He barely looked at me, and he said in a shaky voice "Sit, sit, sit down." I sat down on the edge of the bed not knowing what to say or do. It was completely silent in the room. The television and the radio were off, so the only entertainment was watching him trip out and come down off his high.

It was quite a sight. For ten minutes, I watched him put both his hands on his head, and his eyes moving to the left and right quickly, as if he was watching something move across the room. A couple of times, he removed his hands from his head and grabbed the white sheets tightly, while he moved his head slowly from side to side. He started blinking his eyes slowly, and the head movement began to slow down. He was coming off his high. His words were becoming clearer when he spoke.

"Do you need something?" I said.

"Yeah, could you go into the kitchen and get me some Hennessey," he said.

As I was walking to the kitchen, I was thinking to myself, "He really does not need anymore substance in him, but I sure do." I made me a big glass of straight Hennessey, and I don't even drink Hennessey, but at that time I needed it!

I walked back in the room and handed Mr. Limp his glass. "Thanks how are you?" he asked.

"I'm cool, but the question is how are you? Are you okay?"

"Oh that. I'm fine, just a little high. Do you smoke, you want some?"

"Ah no, I only drink," I said.

"Come sit next to me," he requested. I sat next to him on the bed, and he put his hand on my thigh. He had his other hand under the covers, touching himself trying to get his dick hard. I was just sitting there watching him and drinking the Hennessey. I did not want to sleep with him at all, because I was so turned off by the Crack. He kept on trying to get it up. He was stroking it up and down, and shaking it, but it was not working. Was it the drugs that caused his dick to stay limp, or did he just need a woman's touch? I was curious to know the answer, so I pulled the sheet down to his knees, and I took his tallywacker in my hand. I began to stroke it up and down slowly for a minute or two, but no such luck, it was still soft. I stroked it faster, thinking that would work. I stroked it as fast as I could. I stroked the head of it, and then the base of it, but nothing was working. His thick dick was limp in my hand, flopping around. Even after a woman's touch, it still would not get hard. It was the drugs that were causing the problem.

I took my hand off him, and whispered, "It's not getting hard."

"It's not your fault, its cool." He reached toward the nightstand and picked up the pipe and placed the rock cocaine in it. He put the pipe between his lips, and he flicked the lighter and put the flame directly on the crack. Then, he inhaled the harsh chemical. He held it in for a few seconds, and next he blew the smoke out. He looked at me, and again offered, "Are you sure you don't want some?"

"No, I'm straight."

He took a few more hits, and he put the pipe and the lighter back on the nightstand. All of a sudden, he grabbed his head again, and he mumbled, "The spirits, the spirits."

"What are you talking about?" I said.

"The spirits in room, in room." He pointed straight ahead, and tried to say something, but I had no idea what the hell he was talking about. He just kept pointing straight ahead, saying, "Put down, put it down, down."

So I got off his bed, and walked over to where he was pointing. I started pointing to every object one by one, asking him, "Is this it, you want me to put this down?"

He just shook his head back and forth while grabbing it, and telling me no. When I touched the tall CD tower, he nodded his head up and down. Finally, I figured it out. I laid it on the floor, and he immediately stopped saying the damn spirits were in the room.

He still was tripping out and looking around the room, as if he was watching something move in the room. He was freaking me out, so I said to myself, "I have got to get the hell out of here, before the spirits start telling me to get out." I decided that I should leave, while he was still high. Maybe he wouldn't even notice that I was gone. While he was clenching the bed sheets, I grabbed my purse, and I walked out the door.

That whole scene was crazy and scary. I did not know what to say or do. I was afraid if I made a sudden move that he would freak out. He was seeing spirits in the room, so I did not want to speak. I was afraid that he would think I was one of the spirits and he might attack me. So I just sat there on the bed, drinking a lot, trying to be still and quiet, waiting for the right time to leave.

I was so glad to get out of there. His bodyguard asked me if I was coming back, and I told him, "Hell no."

I cannot even rate the sexual experience, since there was none, but the whole evening was a zero. He was a junkie who could not get it up!

CHAPTER 11
Question and Answers

I made my decision to write this book, based on the reaction that I have received from many different women. There would be times when we were watching a television program or looking in a magazine, and they would see a celebrity they have fantasized about, and their reaction would be, "Look at him, he is so cute, and I just love him." They would also say, "I have the biggest crush on him, I would love to have one night with him." When I would turn and look at them and then tell them that I'd slept with him before, there reaction was always the same. "What, you have got to be kidding! What was he like? You have to tell me everything! Where did you meet him, and how did you hook up with him?"

Women would get so excited and curious to know that here was someone that had experienced it first hand; and I could tell them exactly what it was like, detail by detail. I could satisfy their curiosity. Most women do fantasize and wonder what it would be like to sleep with a particular celebrity. They want to know how it feels when he touches them, how they kiss, and if they can truly satisfy them. I wrote this book because I wanted to try and fulfill their fantasies and dreams.

I have slept with many of the hottest singers, actors, and rappers, more than the nine I wrote about. Some of you may want to know why I slept with so many of them. Well, I really wasn't trying to sleep with as many as I could, that was not my plan. It just seemed to happen that way. I was often around them at the clubs, their houses, or on the set of a show's taping. We were always partying and drinking, just having a good time and enjoying each other's company. If I felt like having sex with one of them, then I would. Both of us knew what we were doing, and we wanted to have some great sex. Besides, I was single, I wanted to do it, and I was having fun. Sex to me is very enjoyable. I would have a good time doing it, and I was never ashamed of it. As long as I was having safe sex, I was okay. I wasn't looking for a relationship with any of them. It was all about hanging out with them, having a good time, and doing what I wanted to do.

Would I change anything about my past? No, not a thing, I loved every minute of it. I was having the time of my life. I truly had a lot of fun. I enjoyed riding in the limos and inviting my girls to come with me. I also loved to make them happy by hooking them up with someone with whom they have always wanted to have sex. I was attending the best parties in the entertainment industry. I was hanging out with the hottest, richest celebrities. I was partying in the VIP areas, drinking Cristal, meeting new people, eating good food, going on shopping sprees, and having great sex with no strings attached.

One of my friends asked me if I was concerned what people would think of me once they read that I slept with so many different celebrities. My answer was, "No, not at all."

Why should I let other people's opinions affect my life or my decisions on how to live it? They are just other people, and it is only their opinions, not mine. Other people do not pay my bills, and they have no outcome in my everyday life. The one thing that I do not care about is what people think of me. I do not let negative thoughts cloud my head. Everyone is always going to have something to say about other people, whether it is good or bad.

Another question I was frequently asked was how I got to meet so many celebrities. It all started when I was with one of my friends, and she introduced me to Dave Brown who gave the hottest parties in Los Angeles, also known as the DB's. Dave and I ended up exchanging phone numbers. He would call me up and invite me to his parties that he was having.

When I would get there, he would always introduce me to his celebrity friends. Most of them that I did meet, would ask for my phone number. Then that celebrity would call and invite me to his party. When I would attend that event, I would get introduced to more celebrities, and I would exchange phone numbers with them. All my friends, with whom I would hang out, looked very good. So we could just be standing around talking amongst ourselves, and one of the celebrities would come up to us and start talking. Phone numbers would get exchanged, and now we had more connections. Sometimes, one of my friends would call me up and ask me if I wanted to go with them to a pool party at a mansion that one of her celebrity friends was having. When I got there, I would end up meeting more of them. Just about every time I got my hair done at Chuck Taylor's on La Cienega Boulevard, I would see someone that played in the NBA. That was always a good place to meet them and still is. All I had to do is be in there the afternoon the day before a game, and they would be there getting their hair cut by Chuck.

Quite a few times, my girls and I would go to the Mondrian Hotel on Sunset Boulevard just to have a drink at the Skybar, and we would meet some of them there. They would be sitting down having a drink with their crew, and they would come over to us and buy us a drink. Hotel bars are a good way to meet them. If there is a major event going on in Los Angeles, like the awards, or an all-star basketball event, just go to the bar area of the hotel the same weekend that the event is taking place, and there will be many of them having a cocktail. My favorite is the W Hotel in Westwood. Many of them stay there. I did mention other hotels they stay at throughout the book. Once you're in that circle of celebrities, and if you look good, it is not hard to do it. I did not sleep with everyone I met. A lot of them were just strictly friends that I would hang out with, or just call and say hi. This is basically how I was able to meet and become friends with them.

Why I decided to leave their names out? I wanted my book to be different. It needed to be entertaining and challenging. I want the readers to have fun and try to figure out who I am talking about. I gave you enough clues to help you realize which celebrities I wrote about, without actually coming out and saying who they are. I made an exception with Chapter 10 because the subject matter was too personal. Some clues are in the names of the chapters, others are the initials of their names. I gave you their heights, eye colors, teams they played for etc…I am sure some of you will know exactly to whom I am referring, especially the ladies who are still hanging around in the industry. You may assume that I am talking about a particular person, but I might not be referring to him at all. Maybe you do know whom I am talking about. If not, just think it is whoever you want it to be. Yes, it probably would be more interesting if I would tell you, but the whole point of my book is to let you know what it is like to sleep with a celebrity. Since my stories are true, you can take your own fantasies that you may have, and use my scenarios to fulfill your fantasies.

Do I still sleep with these celebrities? No, not any more. The reason why I stopped sleeping with them is because I met a really nice man with whom I fell in love. He came into my life, and he treated me like no other man has treated me before. He was very caring to my needs. He treated me the way that I have always wanted a man to treat me. Some men would give me a little of this, and others would only give me a little of that. For example, Mr. A might hold my hand when we were in public, but he would not open the door for me. Mr. B would open the door for me, but he would not hold me while we slept. The man that came into my life absolutely adored me. He gave me everything that I was looking for in a man.

At that time, when he came into my life, I was still out there partying and having a good time. I was only sleeping with him, but he still was not happy with me going out. He ended up giving me an ultimatum. It was either the clubs or him. I had to make a decision.

Well, the decision was not that hard. Of course, I chose him. The only things that I was really getting from partying were some free drinks, money, and some good sex. I could get that from him and a whole lot more, like a lifetime of happiness with someone who truly loved me for who I am, not what I was. We are still together as of this day. We are married. We have a big house, nice cars, and a child together. Life is great!

Printed in the United States
112181LV00002B/3/A